THE WAYWARD GIRL

M.P. STARKWEATHER

PHOENIX ECLIPSE PUBLISHING

I want to dedicate this book to my two biggest fans, my husband Josh and my son Thom, who will probably never read any of my books. Thanks for pushing me to chase my dream. I love you both to the moon and back.

Author's Note

Some of the themes in this book may be triggering to some people. Please be aware that this story includes **death, mention of past infertility, mention of past abortion, demons, detailed sex with multiple partners, and murder.**

Please take your mental health into consideration, and don't read this if any of the things listed above are triggering for you.

ACKNOWLEDGMENTS

I would like to thank:

My author besties, who encourage me to keep writing, even when it's hard;

My amazing PA, Gwen, who is my twinsie;

My Alpha Team who tries hard to keep me on track;

My Editing Team who does their best to make sure my books make sense and have as few typos as possible;

My Cover Artist, Wallflower Designs, who's responsible for the gorgeous images on the front of this book

and My ARC Team, who catch some of the things the rest of us miss.

contents

PROLOGUE

HOW DID I GET HERE?

KENDALL

THE BRIGHT LIGHT SURROUNDING me fades, and I realize that I'm standing in my bedroom. Something seems off about that. Wasn't I just in the back yard? A wave of dizziness washes over me, and I realize that I must have blacked out again. It's happening more and more lately, and I'm becoming increasingly concerned.

Turning the dark metal ring on my index finger, I let my body drop onto my bed. How many hours did I lose this time? The curtains are drawn, and the lights are off. Sunlight streams through the split in the material hanging over the window.

I close my eyes for a moment before shaking away the dizzy feeling and getting to my feet. After stretching for a moment, I turn and leave the room, heading down the stairs into the kitchen.

"Kendall Shaw! Where have you been? You disappeared two days ago, and we searched everywhere! Are you okay? Was this some kind of sick joke?" My roommate, Anna, is clearly not pleased. With her explanation of events, I completely understand her feelings.

"Two days? Where did I go?" I wonder out loud. "What the fuck is happening to me?"

"That's exactly what I just asked you. Where have you been?" she snaps at me again.

"I wish I knew," I reply. I know it's going to make her angrier, but I don't know what's going on, so I can't give her the answers she wants. Anna throws her hands in the air and storms off, muttering to herself. My thumb worries the cool metal of the ring on my index finger once more as the bright light surrounds me.

⁂

As the light fades, I see that I'm in my bedroom again. How did I get here? I was in the kitchen. Something is wrong. I feel strange; off somehow. I can't explain it. I should find Anna and ask if she can take me to the hospital. I should probably see a doctor for these blackouts.

I walk downstairs and a strange sense of déjà vu comes over me. Glancing around, I can see that Anna has changed things up a bit. Perhaps taking my pictures down and getting rid of my decorations is her way of telling me that she's kicking me out.

"I can't stay here anymore, not after what happened," she says. Anna is leaving? Then why is my stuff gone?

I follow her voice into the living room, where she's sitting on the couch. The room is crowded, and I notice that everyone here is connected to me somehow. Co-workers, classmates, old friends—even my second cousin, Carl. This is odd, for sure.

"Is this some kind of intervention, Anna?" I ask, walking over to her. She ignores me completely, as if I'm not standing beside her trying to have a conversation. It seems weird to me that no one will look at me, even as I wave at them.

"Anna, I said I was sorry. I have no idea what's going on. Please don't ignore me," I plead with her. She doesn't respond; won't even lift her head to look at me.

"Where will you go?" an older man asks. Dennis? Why is Dennis here? My boss has never been to my house before. It seems strange for him to be here, but I can't quite grasp why his question to Anna seems significant.

"Oh, hey, Dennis. What's going on?" I try greeting him, but he stares right through me, focusing on Anna. This is getting more and more strange. Why is everyone ignoring me? "Are you guys that mad at me about what has to be a medical condition? This is ridiculous."

"Home. My parents have the basement cleaned out for me. I'll stay there until I can find somewhere else." I have the thought again, *if Anna is moving out, why is all my stuff gone?*

Dennis sits down beside her and takes her hand. "I don't blame you. I wouldn't be able to stay here after what happened either. How did her parents take the news?"

Anna wipes at the tears I hadn't noticed. Why is she crying? What the fuck are they talking about? Glancing around the room, I notice that everyone here is dressed in muted colors. If I didn't know better, I would think this was a wake, or a funeral reception. It can't be, right? I'm not dead. I'm standing right here.

"Obviously, they were shocked. No one expects their daughter to drop dead at twenty-six on the kitchen floor. I think it was worse because she hadn't talked to them in a while. Mr. and Mrs. Shaw were devastated when I called them. They sent someone to pick up her stuff. Mrs. Shaw couldn't leave DC because of work." Anna wipes her eyes again. "I just can't believe Kendall is gone."

"I'm not gone. Anna, I'm standing right in front of you," I insist, reaching for her hand. My hand moves right through hers as if it's nothing. She shivers, like the contact, or lack of, sent a cold chill up her arm. What the fuck is going on here? I start to panic, then realize that my heart should be racing, and I should be breathing hard. But it's not, and I'm not.

Realization starts to set in. I'm dead. Holy shit; *I'm dead.* Not only that, but I'm a ghost. I fly toward the front door, pausing to turn the knob before remembering that it won't work. I push through the door and stand on the porch. If I died here, am I trapped in this house forever?

There's only one way to find out. I stomp down the steps to the edge of the sidewalk. Mustering all my courage, I step off the curb and into the road. Within a moment, I'm in my bedroom again. Great. I can't leave. I wonder for a second what will happen to me when Anna moves out.

Will someone else buy the house? We had just talked our landlord into selling it to us on contract. Fuck. I feel awful for Anna, but there's nothing I can do to help her.

Will I be alone forever? I've read books and seen movies like this before. If I can figure out what unfinished business I have, I'll be able to take care of it and move on.

But I'm only twenty-six. All of my business is unfinished. I haven't had a chance to do anything yet, and now I never will.

The next few days seem to pass in a blur. I learn more about my death, and about being a ghost. I died suddenly; Anna found me in the kitchen. My eyes were glassy, and I was cold.

I hear her on the phone with someone, telling them about the nightmares that plague her now. She insists that getting out of this house will help her to forget about me. I hate the idea that I've caused her pain, but I don't want to be forgotten.

As for being a ghost—apparently, I don't need sleep. I can't be seen or heard. And since I can't interact with anything, I spend all my time bored unless Anna watches TV or uses the computer.

Everything I own is gone. I guess I don't need any of it anyway. Anna must have packed it all up for my parents. Why they'd want my belongings is beyond me. Neither of them was too concerned when I moved out. It's not like we were close. But the Shaws were always more worried about public opinion than family anyway. After all, you can't run for Congress if your daughter is a screw up who doesn't have her life together. Better to just let her leave. I wonder if my death will help with the re-election campaign. It's not like I'll find out, unless Anna takes up an interest in politics in the near future.

Being estranged from them actually helped my mother's cause. I don't assume that I'm the reason she got elected, but I know that using our lack of a relationship definitely got her sympathy. The sad thing is that I can't even been upset with her about it. She has some great ideas and would make an amazing President someday. I just wish she'd cared half as much about her daughter as she does about the rest of the country.

I don't know how many days pass before Anna has all of her stuff packed. I just know that one day, she starts loading a truck with boxes and bags. As pointless as it is, I do my best to get in her way. I want her to acknowledge that she's leaving me here. But nothing I do matters. Anna and the movers walk right through me when I block the door.

There's no way for me to shut and lock the front door, so I can't physically stop her. I scream as they walk through me, leaving me behind. I try to follow, not wanting to be alone, but every time, I'm zapped back into my empty bedroom. No matter which direction I go, no matter what my intent, I find myself back in that lonely space where I must have died.

It's weird; I don't feel dead. Of course, I have no idea what dead is supposed to feel like, so I guess I wouldn't really know.

With Anna gone, I have nothing to do. There's nothing to distract me from my thoughts, my regrets. I let the emotions wash over me, unable to do anything to stop them. Without a physical body, I can't cry. I can't beat my fists against the wall or hurt myself by breaking a mirror.

Defeat sets in, and I spend more time under the old tree in the back yard. The squirrels don't seem to mind me; one even chatters at me as if I can understand him. We watch the seasons change together before he tucks into the tree to hibernate. The cold doesn't bother me, and I have no motivation to leave my spot under the tree, so I stay there for all of the first winter.

I ignore the realtors who come and lead people through the house. I push away the emotions that constantly attempt to rip me apart, reminding me of everything I'll never have. Loneliness is my constant companion. I try to keep up with how many days and weeks pass, but I can't.

Wandering the house and yard becomes my every day. Sometimes I sing, other times I scream. When that becomes tiresome, I mourn everything I've lost. I've always heard that your life passes in front of your eyes when you die. Turns out, that happens after you die—when you're trying to figure out what's keeping your soul trapped in this torturous pain.

It's not like I hurt physically. No, this is much worse. I could handle physical pain. This is gut-wrenching emotional damage that doesn't stop. I can't cry it out and move on. It's just there. Constantly. There is no relief, no comfort in knowing that there's a light at the end of the tunnel, an end to my pain. Instead, I have no one and nothing.

Days pass slowly and quickly. I'm thankful that I've already died, because if I were stuck here alive, I would find a way to end my suffering. I don't know how much more of this I can take. There has to be a way to make it all stop, but I can't find it.

Watching my memories, searching for a way out of here, it all becomes pointless. I never learn anything that helps. I work on forgiving my family, thinking that maybe that will set me free. I convince myself that they did the best they could, and yet I'm still here.

Snow thaws, and storms come in the spring. I never liked the rain when I was alive, but now, I wish for it. The booming thunder and crack of lightning distracts me from the hell I'm in. With nothing to look forward to, I find myself letting go. The memories assault me, but I pay them no mind. The seasons change, and I'm still here. The house needs upkeep, but no one comes around. I wonder if it's because they can feel me here. Or if what happened was just too tragic, and they can't handle thinking about it.

I may never know the truth of it.

CHAPTER ONE

NEW ROOMMATES

FIVE YEARS LATER

KENDALL

AFTER ANNA MOVED OUT, I lost track of time. Days and nights ran together, and I have no idea how long I've been dead, or how long I've been roaming this house alone. I spend my days exploring the small, fenced-in yard. Sometimes I daydream under the oak tree, or watch the squirrels play. My favorite times have been during the storms. I can stand in the middle of the yard, in the pouring rain with thunder and lightning, and I don't have to worry about getting hit. I don't even get wet.

I'm sure at some point my birthday has come and gone, but without Anna here, I don't know how many years I've been a ghost. How many birthdays have I missed? You'd think the idea of not aging would comfort me, but instead, I'm angry. Why am I stuck here, alone and miserable? More than anything, I want to leave the property, but no matter how many times I try, I find myself back in the room that was once mine.

At least someone took down that ugly sign from the front of the house. McMahan Realty. They could have tried harder to sell the house. If they had just fixed it up a little, someone would have wanted it. Instead, I've watched as it falls more and more into disrepair. I guess the realtor finally gave up and took the sign down. It's not like anyone has been here recently to even look at the house.

Right after Anna left, there were people and open houses. It was very crowded in my house, but no one stayed. That didn't last long, though, and I've been alone ever since. Moving through the walls and floating around the house becomes like second nature to me. I still try to play with the dark band on my index finger, but it no longer moves the way it used to.

In the back yard, leaning against the oak tree, I watch the squirrels fight over something when a noise gets my attention. I remember that noise but can't quite place it. I can tell it's coming from out front, so I pop out there to see what's going on.

"Are you sure about this place, Jack?" a dark-haired, blue-eyed man asks another.

The blond man looks back at him and nods. "I'm sure. It's a great investment, Spence. And we can do all the work ourselves."

Spence doesn't say anything, but locks eyes with me. Can he actually see me? If so, why isn't he saying anything? "If you're sure," he responds. I stand there, dumbfounded, as I watch them each grab a backpack from the truck and head up the steps and into my house.

Jack walks past me without so much as a nod in recognition. Spence can't seem to take his eyes off me. "Can you see me?" I ask him. His eyes snap up to meet mine, but he doesn't respond. He can hear me too! This is amazing. I just have to get him away from his friend and I won't be alone anymore.

"What time is Murr heading over?" Jack asks Spence as they walk through the front door. I follow them, because this is the most excitement I've had in years. I desperately want to know what's happening here.

"He'll be over when he gets off work. He's gotta stop at his mom's to pick up the last of his stuff," Spence responds.

"Then I guess we get first pick of the bedrooms," Jack insists. I follow them upstairs, hoping I can convince Spence to take my room.

"Spence, take this one. Please. I haven't had anyone to talk to in forever." If I were still alive, I would have felt my face flush at how forward I'm being, but I'm dead, so it's not like we're gonna hook up.

His eyes meet mine and he shakes his head. My heart sinks. I guess I should consider that he won't want to be friends with the ghost in his new home. I force myself to go transparent and watch him sigh in relief. It hurts when he chooses Anna's old room for himself.

Feeling his rejection harder than I should, I focus on disappearing. I can't actually leave the property, but right now, I want to be invisible. After a few minutes, I see Spence relax, which tells me I've managed to make myself vanish from his view. Good. I can use this when I need to.

I watch as Jack debates between my room and the one we used as a den when Anna and I lived here. Disappointment fills me up when he selects mine and drops his bag inside the door. "This one is bigger than the other one. Murr should have figured out how to get here earlier if he doesn't like it," Jack says. I pull myself back together, making my form as close to solid as I can manage, but Jack still doesn't seem to see me.

At one point, he walks right through me while carrying boxes into his new room. He doesn't even flinch, even though I see Spence shiver. I wonder why Spence is keeping this a secret. I want to ask him, but I'm sure he won't talk to me after the way he avoided selecting my room for his own.

With boxes stacked along the walls of nearly every room, I start to wonder how much more stuff these guys could possibly have. Then they start moving furniture in. A few hours later, another man arrives, and I realize this is Murr.

"Damnit, Jack, I knew I'd end up with the smallest bedroom," he says to the blond. I laugh, and for a moment, Murr looks in my direction. I don't think he can see me, but he seems to sense that I'm here. This could work for me. He seems less spooked than Spence is by my presence.

"Hey, Jack. Spence. Have you guys noticed any weird shifts in the energy of this place since you started moving stuff in?" Murr asks. Is he actually going to acknowledge that he feels me here? I do a giddy little dance, then realize that Spence is staring at me again.

"I haven't noticed anything," Spence says, still watching me. Why is he lying to his friends? Is he ashamed of his ability? We're going to have to talk about this later.

Jack shakes his head. "Me neither, Murr. It's probably just you. I never should have told you about that hottie who died here."

Hottie? Is he talking about me? I wonder when they saw me or heard about what happened here. "I can't believe her parents sold the place so cheap. I would have expected it to go for double what we paid," Spence says, still looking right at me. Is he trying to tell me what happened?

"You bought the house from my parents? How? They didn't own it when I died," I insist. I have so many questions about everything, and I don't think I'll ever get answers.

"When I heard that her parents bought the place, I thought that was weird. But after talking to them, I understand why they did it," Jack says.

"Weren't they trying to keep it out of the hands of that film crew?" Murr adds. Film crew? What are they talking about? I turn my attention to Spence, because I know he's my best chance of finding out what all this means.

"Yeah, the one that wanted to make a 'mockumentary' about the girl's life and how her parents abused and neglected her until she ran away," Spence explains.

"What? None of that is true," I say. At this point, I'm grateful that he's explaining things, but even more confused about what's been happening. How did I miss all of that? "How long have I been dead?" I don't expect him to answer.

"I can't believe how much this house has gone downhill in the past five years," Spence says, emphasizing the five. I've been gone for five years. I realize that I've spent most of that time here alone. It feels weird to not be alone anymore.

"Thank you," I say to Spence. "I can't handle any more today, but thank you for giving me some answers." He nods almost imperceptibly, and I poof myself into the back yard. I can't take any more news of the past five years. I need some time to process.

❊⊱❊⊱Ⅹ⊰❊⊰❊

MURRAY

"Spence, are you sure you don't feel that? It's like the whole mood of the house changed," I ask, knowing that he's seen something he's not talking about.

"I'm sure. Look, Murr, I know you're sensitive to energy, but there's nothing here to worry about," he answers. Jack stares at him before turning his attention on me.

"Do you think this place is haunted?" he asks with a shiver.

"Maybe. I definitely felt something, and I think Spence knows more than he's saying," I offer.

Spence glares at me, then stomps off into his bedroom and slams the door. What's his problem? Jack and I exchange a glance, then get back to unpacking. Who knew we had so much stuff to fill this house?

"I'm gonna check out the back yard while I take a break. Don't forget we still have to get groceries. Spence will try to get out of it again," I say, walking down the stairs. I don't tell Jack, but I'm following the energy signature I sensed when I first arrived. I suspect that the young woman who died here is still hanging around, and I can't wait to find a way to prove it.

Once I'm in the back yard, I notice that the fence is the only thing that's been cared for here. Even the oak tree looks sad. I walk across the yard, sensing the energy I'm searching for. It's stronger here, like she's sitting under the tree, waiting.

"Okay, I'm gonna sound crazy here, but, there's no other way to do this," I start. "I can feel you. I know you're here. I think Spence can see you, but he insists there's nothing here to be afraid of. Either that means he doesn't see you, or he knows you won't hurt us. Either way, I just want you to know that we aren't planning anything nefarious here. We just needed a place to live, and this house was cheap. We'll take good care of it. And you're welcome to stay if you want. I can't see or hear you, but I'm always willing to hang out."

Feeling stupid for standing in the yard talking to a tree, I turn and head back inside. A wave of relief washes over me when I feel the energy following me.

KENDALL

It seems stupid to me that I needed to hear that I'm still welcome in my own home. It's not like I can go anywhere else. But knowing that Murr senses me and is willing to be a friend—well, it helps to ease the loneliness that had settled into my soul. I follow him back into the house and upstairs. Once I realize that each of the guys has shut himself in his own bedroom, I decide that Spence and I need to have a talk.

I would prefer to knock, but I'm not sure how to do that. So, I let myself into his room through the wall, careful to make sure he's decent before I enter.

"Oh, you startled me," he whispers, placing a hand over his heart.

"Sorry. I can't exactly knock. Can we talk?" I ask, hoping that he doesn't scream and run away.

"I guess so. I don't really want the other guys to know I can see you. They already think I'm weird, and I don't want to make it worse," he explains.

"Murr already suspects. He told me as much in the yard. But it's not like I can talk to him, so your secret is safe with me," I insist.

Chapter Two

Adjustments

KENDALL

My afterlife gets a little better after my heart-to-heart with Spence. It turns out that his ability to see and communicate with ghosts completely freaks him out. He has no idea how to deal with it, and the one time he tried to talk to Murr about it, in a hypothetical sense, they ended up fighting because Murr thinks it's way cooler than being able to sense energies.

It takes a few weeks to ease Spence into becoming my friend, but I manage. I no longer try to talk to him when the other guys are around. In exchange, we have long talks twice a week after everyone else is asleep for the night.

As nice as it is to have someone to talk to, I miss physical contact. Spence asks me about that one night, and that leads to an experiment to see if he can touch me. We hold our hands up, palms facing each other. Instead of threading our fingers together and holding hands, mine slides right through his and he shivers. "Well, that didn't work," I say, unable to hide the disappointment in my tone.

"Hey, don't get upset. There has to be a way. We'll figure it out," Spence reassures me.

"It's just been so long, Spence. It's making me crazy. Honestly, I think it was easier when I was here alone." I regret the words as soon as they leave my mouth.

"Oh," he says. "I'm sorry." Before I can say or do anything to apologize, Spence turns the light off and flops onto his bed. Fuck. Will being dead ever get easier? I don't want to be a weirdo, so I excuse myself silently.

This is what you wanted, right? To be alone again. I ask myself. If I was alive, I'd be crying right now. But I'm just a ghost, so I don't have that outlet. I don't have anything anymore. And that's the worst part of it all. If I could move on, at least that would be progress. Being stuck here is miserable.

I spend the next few days avoiding the guys as much as I can. When I catch Spence staring at me, I leave the room.

Murr tracks me down again for another of his 'talks,' which are ridiculous, because I can't respond to anything he says. "Hey, Kendall, it's just me. Oh, that was dumb. You can see me. Sorry, sometimes I forget that part. I noticed your energy has been sad for a few days. I'd love to cheer you up. Would you like to watch a movie with me?"

"And just how would that work, Murr?" I ask, even though he can't hear me.

"I know it sounds weird, but one of my co-workers suggested a rom-com that's new, and I hate watching those alone. I thought maybe it would help cheer you up. Or at least give you something to do besides wandering through the house. I'm gonna go up and start it; if you're interested, just come on up." He turns and walks away, as if I've agreed to join him.

I wonder if he would feel rejected if I didn't go. I already feel bad enough about hurting Spence's feelings; I don't want to do that to Murr too. Sighing, I will myself inside the house, popping up in Murr's room just as he turns the movie on. I think it's sweet how he spends time researching my life and uses my name now. It's almost as if he understands how alone I've felt and wants to make it better.

"Oh, good. You decided to join me." Murr doesn't say another word through the entire movie. We watch in silence, and I have to admit—it's nice to just sit here and enjoy a story that's not mine. Especially since there's so much of mine, I don't know anything about. If I hadn't alienated Spence, I could have asked him to have Murr do more research for me.

When the movie ends, I lean over and press a kiss to Murr's cheek. He shivers and covers the spot with his hand. The blush on his cheeks tells me that he's not used to attention from ladies, or maybe ghosts, I can't be sure. But he did something sweet for me, and I want him to know I appreciate it.

I leave before he can process what just happened, because it would be impossible for us to discuss it. I wander around outside for a while, until I catch Spence watching me. We've been avoiding each other since I hurt his feelings. I guess I should be happy he hasn't tried an exorcism yet to get rid of me. His expression is sad and nearly breaks my heart. When he starts to cross the yard, I turn to go in the opposite direction.

"Please wait, Kendall. I owe you an apology. I don't even care if I look like a crazy person in the back yard, talking to myself. I need to make this right." Spence stares at me, waiting to see if I'm going to take off.

"I'm listening; even if I don't think you're the one who needs to apologize," I respond quietly.

"I shouldn't have gotten shitty with you when you said you were better off alone. I'll admit, it hurt me, and I over-reacted. I'm sorry. Can you forgive me?" he says, not bothering to whisper.

"I'll only forgive you on one condition," I insist, locking eyes with him.

"Anything," he answers.

"You have to forgive me too. I was thoughtless and realize that what I said hurt you, even if it wasn't meant that way."

Spence smiles at me, and the warmth in his eyes touches my soul. For a moment, I feel almost alive again. Before he has a chance to respond, I feel myself being ripped away from him. Everything goes black, and it reminds me of the day I died.

My eyes open, and I'm lying on the floor in my old bedroom. "Who the fuck are you and how did you get in my room?" Jack asks, clearly freaking out.

I sit up, my eyes wide. "You can see me?"

He nods. "Yes, I can see you. You're on the floor in my bedroom. How did you get in here?"

"Honestly, I wish I knew. I was in the back yard talking to Spence, and suddenly I'm here. Why does everything suddenly hurt?" I mutter to myself, not realizing that Jack is hanging on my every word.

"Spence let you in here? I'm gonna kill him. I don't want strangers in my room, even if they're hot," he insists.

I laugh. He obviously has no idea who or what I am. "It's not like that, Jack. I can try to explain, but I'm not sure you'll believe me." Something in his hand catches my attention. I look down at my hand, noticing that the ring he's holding looks exactly like the one on my finger. Is that how he pulled me back here? What the fuck is going on?

"Well, you'd better start talking before I call the cops and have you arrested," he threatens. When I laugh again, he groans, clearly annoyed at my response. "And how do you know my name?"

"You might wanna get Murr and Spence in here for this," I say as I try to compose myself again.

Jack pulls out his phone and types a message, staring at me the whole time. The phone makes a noise, indicating that someone has responded, then chimes again. He stands next to the door with his arms crossed while we wait.

"What the fuck is going on?" Murr asks, looking at Jack like he's crazy. "I thought you said we had an intruder."

Before Jack or I can respond, Spence darts in the door. "Kendall? What happened?" I see the moment he realizes what he's said, because his face turns beet red and he buries his face in his hands. So much for keeping his secret.

"Kendall? What? How?" Murr asks. "Wait, you guys can see her?" Well, this is a complication. I'd expected to be able to talk to all three of them. Shit.

"Damn. I was hoping we'd all be able to talk," I say, looking from Spence to Murr.

Jack stares at me for a moment, then looks at Spence. "What is going on here?"

"I'm not sure I understand it, honestly. This is Kendall. She used to live here, you know, when she was alive," Spence offers.

"She's really here? And you two can see her? How is this shit fair?" Murr yells.

Jack and Spence both nod. "You can't see her?" Jack asks. Murr shakes his head.

"I can sense her energy, but there's no one here but you guys. She's a ghost," he insists.

This isn't going at all the way I'd expected. Of course, I didn't really think Jack would find a way to see me, but here we are.

"Where did you get that ring?" I ask Jack, gesturing to the black metal he's playing with on his finger.

"Not that it's any of your business, but I found it under the bed," he answers, closing his hand around it possessively. Interesting.

"I'm just trying to figure this out. You see," I hold up my hand, showing him the identical ring, I wear. "It looks just like mine, and I wondered if that one was actually the same one, I'm wearing. That could explain how you couldn't see me before, but now you can."

"You don't look like a ghost," Jack insists, stepping closer and holding out a hand to help me up. I hesitate before reaching up and taking his hand. I gasp when my hand doesn't pass through his. Spence steps forward and holds out his hand. When I reach for it, my hand slides right through his.

"This doesn't make any sense," I say aloud, even though I'm talking to myself.

Jack watches as I can't touch Spence, and he jumps back, letting go of my hand. I stumble before getting my footing. How can I touch Jack, but not Spence? And why can't Murr see me? This is insane. Murr steps forward, putting his hand on Jack's shoulder.

"I have a theory. Can I see that ring?" he asks, holding out his hand.

Jack hesitates for a moment, then hands it over. I know the instant that Jack can no longer see me and Murr can. It has to be the ring.

"Holy shit, this is awesome," Murr says, staring at the ring on his finger.

"Where did she go?" Jack asks at the same time.

Murr holds out a hand to me. "It's nice to finally meet you, Kendall." I take his hand, marveling at the feeling of his hand against mine. I giggle when he pulls my hand up and kisses the back of it. Who knew I was into that?

"It's nice to meet you, too. This is really weird, though," I admit.

"Is she still here? What's she saying? Give me my ring back," Jack interrupts.

"Hang on, man. I think we each should get a chance to officially meet her," Murr argues, handing the ring to Spence.

As soon as the ring touches his hand, I walk over and pull Spence into a hug. I start to cry when my arms don't go through him, and he hugs me back. "It's been so long," I whisper.

"It won't have to stay that way," he whispers back.

"So, it's definitely the ring. But apparently, Spence can see and talk to her without it," Murr hypothesizes.

"Which means I should keep it, because you can sense her. So, you both have a connection that I don't," Jack argues.

CHAPTER THREE

RESEARCH

JACKSON

THE ARGUMENT ABOUT THE ring isn't settled, even after two weeks. None of us wants to give up the ability to see, hear, and touch Kendall. I wouldn't have ever expected to fall for a ghost, but I'm pretty sure that's what's happening here. And as much as I don't like to share, I'm not even jealous of my friends having feelings for her, too.

We share the ring equally, switching daily, or whenever Kendall needs to talk to someone besides the person with it. "Have I mentioned that I hate research?" I grumble, scrolling through articles on my laptop while Murr looks through a stack of books from the library.

"It doesn't matter if you hate it; we have to do this for Kendall. We have to find a way to help her," Murr insists.

"Do you really think that she's actually alive? I mean, they had a funeral and buried her body five years ago," I explain. "It's not like she has a body to go back into. You realize that, right? What exactly can we do to help her, besides sending her into the light?"

I'm pissed that there's really nothing we can do, and I don't want to admit how much I really want her to be able to stay. And I'm an asshole, even if that's not my intent.

"Way to go, dick. Kendall heard that, and now she's run off," Spence says from the door.

Shit. It's Spence's day with the ring, so of course, I don't know where Kendall is. "I didn't mean it the way it sounded." There's no point in defending myself, and I know it, but guilt settles in my chest and I try anyway.

"Give me the ring; I'll go find her," Murr offers, holding out his hand.

"It should be me. I'm the one who fucked up; let me fix it," I suggest, holding out my hand.

SPENCER

"There is no way I'm giving either of you this ring right now. It's my turn, and I'll take care of it. I just wanted you to know that she heard you. We have to be more careful about what we say if we're not the one who can see her," I insist. I don't wait for either of them to respond, turning and walking out the door.

I don't tell them that I know where she's going. With all our conversations, we've discussed nearly the entire five years she's been trapped here. I know Kendall better than the other guys do, even without the ring that allows me to touch her.

Sure enough, she's curled up under the tree in the back yard. "Kendall, sweetie, it's just me," I say softly as I pick her up and set her in my lap. If the neighbors are watching, they'll think I'm looney for sure, but now is not the time to care about other people's opinions.

"He's right," she says between dry sobs. It's weird to me that the dead can't cry. It should be weirder to me that I'm in love with a ghost, but it's not. I know the other guys feel the same way, and I don't care. Kendall is ours, and I will not let Jack ruin that.

"Jack is an ass. He didn't mean it. Please, baby, look at me," I plead with her. But she buries her face in my neck and holds onto me as if I'm the only thing keeping her from floating away. And maybe I am. I don't know how being dead works. Is she stuck here because she died traumatically? Or is she here because of unfinished business? No clue. But if there's a chance that Jack's words can make her disappear, I'm going to do everything I can to stop it.

I place my finger under her chin and tilt her head up to look at me. Our eyes lock, and I see how badly Jack's careless words have hurt her. Without thinking, I press my lips to hers, wanting nothing more than to comfort my girl.

The kiss quickly turns feral, as she takes control, straddling me and dipping her tongue into my mouth. I will give her whatever she needs, with no regrets. Anything I have that will make her feel better; I offer it with no strings attached. My heart is hers.

KENDALL

Jack's words hurt me, but he's right. I have no physical body to go back to. By now, my body is all but disintegrated. It's been five years. Five long, painful, lonely years. I spent so much time alone that it physically hurt me, even though I don't have a body. I guess it hurt my soul.

I can't go back to feeling that loneliness constantly, even if the alternative is letting Jack's words hurt me. When Spence kisses me, I lose control. Before I realize what I'm doing, I straddle him and start grinding as I deepen the kiss. If our roles were reversed, I'd have to be concerned about not getting consent. But I'm a ghost, so that doesn't matter, right?

The moment I have the thought, I break the kiss. Of course, consent matters. Even if I'm not corporeal, I can't just take what I want without asking if it's what he wants too. "I'm so sorry, Spence. I shouldn't have done that." My apology sounds insincere, but I hope he understands that I'm still pretty worked up from dry humping him.

"Kendall, baby, you never have to apologize to me for anything. I'm yours. Use me however you need to. Do whatever makes you feel better," Spence says before pressing his lips to mine again. This man, I swear if I was still alive, he'd be the death of me. And you would not hear a single complaint from me about it. I would die happy.

His kisses are nearly enough to make me forget Jack's thoughtless words. Nearly. When he pulls away, the words rush back at me.

"Thank you," I say, pressing my forehead to Spence's. "But Jack is right. I don't have a body to go back into. There's nothing you guys can do to help me. Unless it's helping me move on. And I don't want that anymore. I thought I did, but then I met you guys."

"Kendall, baby, you can't give up," he insists.

"Spence, there's nothing you can do. We should just enjoy what we have and let the rest go," I say, my heart aching for more than stolen moments.

He pulls me close and kisses me again, this time not holding back. His hands trail down my body, and I think he's decided to show me exactly what he wants. Unfortunately, the nosey neighbor chooses this moment to butt in.

"Spencer? Are you having a seizure?" Mrs. Jones calls to him over the fence. I turn my head and see her face barely visible over the top of the wooden privacy panel. So much for giving us any privacy.

"Oh, no. I totally forgot that no one else can see me. Now I've made you look crazy," I say, sliding off his lap.

"Meet me in my room. We're not done with this," he says, barely moving his mouth, before turning to the interruption and smiling cheerfully. "I'm fine, Mrs. Jones. Just dozing off a bit and must have been dreaming. Thanks for the wake-up call."

Spence stands and strolls into the house, not giving the nosey old woman another second of his attention. I close my eyes and poof into Spence's room, making it there before he does. I hear the other guys stop him, asking if I'm okay. I don't catch his response, but a minute later, he bursts through his door with a feral expression. The door slams and, with a flick of his wrist, it locks behind him.

"Where were we?" he asks, stalking over to me as if he's the hunter and I'm the prey. It's hot, and I'm more into it than I thought I ever would be.

I flop back onto his bed and wait for him to join me. I have no idea how or if this will work, even with the ring, but I want Spence to touch me; I want him inside of me. These men make me feel things that I don't remember ever feeling before, or since my death. And I don't want any of it to stop.

He pounces on me, capturing my lips with his and pinning me to the bed beneath him. I fist my hands in his hair, moaning against his mouth as our tongues tangle together. His hands roam over me, the sensation too much and not enough at the same time.

I push him back, and he stops, thinking he's gone too far. Spence's eyes go wide when I pull my tank top over my head and drop it to the floor, exposing myself to him. I drag him back on top of me, shifting so we're side by side now, giving him more access to touch me. We kiss again, rough and needy.

Then Spence trails his lips down my jaw, nibbling at my neck as he gingerly cups my breasts. "More, Spence. I'm not breakable. Please. I need you to be rough with me," I insist. His only response is a growl before he bites down on my neck and pinches my nipples. I moan in pleasure, loving the jolt of desire that courses through me at his touch. "Yes, like that. I need you, Spence."

I know that begging is not a good look here, but I can't stop myself. I'm desperate for him to keep going. I want to feel his hands and mouth everywhere. He kisses down my collarbone before catching a nipple between his teeth. After flicking it with his tongue, he sucks it into his mouth hard. I nearly come from that alone, but I want more. It's been so long since I've been touched, and I find that I'm starved for it.

Sitting up, I reach between us and unfasten my jeans, struggling to get them off while he's worshipping my breasts with his hands, tongue and teeth. When I'm bared before him, I can't help sliding a hand between my legs and marveling at how wet I am. Maybe this will work after all.

I grab the hem of his shirt, dragging it over his head. Spence helps me take his jeans and boxers off, and I stare at his erection in amazement. It's not like I've never seen a cock before, but it's been so long. And I'm pretty sure he's larger than average, though I don't have much experience to judge by.

Wrapping my hand around his girth, I pull him toward my mouth. He surprises me by flipping me over and pulling me on top of him. The moment his tongue laps at my clit, I suck his dick into my mouth. I've never done this before, but it's hot as fuck. I try to focus on licking and sucking him while he distracts me with his mouth on my pussy.

I come on his tongue, crying out with my first orgasm. "Spence, I want you. Please." He groans against my center before flipping me over to face him.

"Are you sure? This isn't something we can take back once it's done," he says softly. The concern this man has for me melts my heart.

Instead of responding, I rub myself against him, locking my eyes with his until he can't hold back anymore. "Fuck, Kendall. You're killing me. Take whatever you want from me," Spence says through gritted teeth. I can tell he's struggling to maintain control. I want to see him lose it, for me.

I slide back up his cock, then slam myself down on it, my ass slapping against his balls. "Oh, Spence," I cry out, being stretched more than I can ever remember. For a moment I freeze, and he seems to understand.

"It's okay, baby. Take a breath; good girl. Now you have to move, or it's just gonna hurt more," he encourages. When I start to ride him, he continues to praise me. "Oh, yes, that's it. Mmm, just like that. You're so perfect. So tight. I love the way you grip me while you ride my cock."

It doesn't take long for my next orgasm to hit, sending him over the edge with me.

CHAPTER FOUR

MAKING UP

KENDALL

THERE'S NO POINT IN worrying about birth control or diseases. I wonder if I should have said something about that, or if Spence just assumed. I mean, I'm already dead, so I doubt I'm susceptible to either one at this point. And there's no need for me to clean up, either. It's strange, but I'm okay with it. Even if I wasn't, it's not like I could do anything about it.

Spence pulls me down for a long, lazy kiss. I sink into him, enjoying the physical closeness I've done without for so long. As much as I never want this to end, I know it has to. We can't stay like this forever. He's alive, and I'm not. There's no happy ending for this situation.

I back away, climbing off the bed and getting dressed quickly. I should tell him that this can't happen again. There's no future in it for him, and it's not fair. To either of us. Sure, I'll have to nurse my heartache when it ends, but if he tries to hold on to me, it'll be far worse for him.

"What's wrong, baby?" It's as if this man can see into my soul, and I'm not sure how to feel about it.

I can't stop myself from speaking my mind when he looks at me like he's half in love already. "Spence, you know that this isn't going to end happily for us, right? I'm dead, and you're not."

"We'll figure that part out. Don't worry," he says with a cocky grin. I shake my head and drop a kiss on his lips before I let myself fade away again. I need a little time to myself, and that means I'll have to avoid Spence and Murr.

Part of me feels bad for Jack, since he's the only one who can't see me without the ring. What is the deal with that fucking ring? Did it kill me? Or is it just the thing that's holding my spirit here? I need to figure this out.

JACKSON

I'm a dick. A complete and total asshole. If Kendall never spoke to me again, I would deserve that punishment for the stupid and thoughtless things I said. I mean, having the thoughts is one thing, but saying them without making sure she wasn't in ear shot was careless.

I should just take the ring from Spence and go find her to apologize. Maybe if I admit that I'm scared we won't be able to help her, she'll forgive me. But I can't do that until I have answers.

Cracking open another dusty book that Murr grabbed from the library, I resign myself to research. As much as I hate it, I'll force myself to do it. For her. Kendall deserves better than what's happened to her. And we all need answers.

I spend a while reading before something catches my eye. "Murr, I think I found something." I look up to find my friend's amber eyes on mine. "This book talks about an enchanted ring that has specific powers." Before this situation, I would have tossed this book aside as fiction. Now I'm not so sure.

"What does it say?" he asks, moving closer to my seat.

"The ring was forged, then enchanted by a witch. It claims that the witch bound a demon to the ring, and that's where the power comes from. This sounds insane, Murr. It can't be true, can it?" I can't help being skeptical about all of this, even if I've seen things I shouldn't be able to.

He shrugs and motions for me to keep talking.

"The witch named it *'Devoted Tempest'* and gave it to her lover. And then it gets weird. The guy died; it's possible the demon ate him? I don't know, Murr. But it's a start." I hand him the book and stand up to stretch. I've been sitting here for far too long.

MURRAY

Reading the book Jack hands me, I can see why he's having trouble believing it all. I mean, who wants to admit that magic and witches are real? Probably only those of us who grew up in families that still follow the old ways. Which means, just me. Spence believes but tries to hide it. He just wants to be normal. I embrace my abilities and hate that he can do more than I can. Honestly, that's just life. We each have our skills, and pining for someone else's won't help matters.

I barely glance up when Jack walks out of the room. I'm consumed by my research. I need these answers as much as I need to breathe.

Armed with more potential info than we had this morning, I start searching everywhere for *'Devoted Tempest'* and anything related to this witch. Within a few hours, I have a better understanding of the ring and its purpose. The witch, who strangely is not named anywhere, had it forged so she could bind her lover to her for eternity. She was concerned that he'd been unfaithful and decided to do something about it.

While I understand her upset, and the desire to have a faithful mate...I have to admit, this bitch was crazy. I mean, creating a ring that would devour your lover's soul if they strayed? That should be the definition of insanity.

Understanding the purpose of the ring is great, but it doesn't tell us how it works, or why it did this to Kendall. She wasn't in a relationship when she died, so it makes no sense. And we have no idea how to reverse it. If we even can. I hate to admit, Jackson made a good point earlier when he said there was nothing for Kendall to come back to. She doesn't have a body, and it's not like we can create one.

There has to be something I'm missing here.

KENDALL

Running away from my feelings for Spence isn't helping, but I can't let myself fall for these guys. It's unfair to them. There aren't a lot of places I can go to be alone, so I hide in the attic. It's dusty, but I don't mind.

The quiet is overbearing and suffocating. Five years of it was too much. As much as I felt like I needed space, I can't stay away from the guys. I've been too lonely, and it hurts too badly.

This is a horrible idea and I know it. Even as I try to talk myself out of it, I seek out the guys. We've gotten close enough since they moved in that I can sense their location as long as they're in the house. Maybe that's the connection to the house, but I like to think it's them.

Murr is reading in the den. He seems completely absorbed in what he's doing, scribbling notes and muttering to himself as he bounces from book to book. I should ask him what he's found, but I'm not sure I want to know yet.

Spence is staring at his ceiling. I hope that I didn't hurt him too much by running away like I did. We'll have to talk about that later. I don't think I can handle that conversation right now.

Jack is sitting on his bed in my old room with his eyes closed. He's not sleeping, though. I can tell from his clenched fists that he's struggling with something. Knowing that he can't see or feel me, I sit on the bed next to him, watching, searching. I want to make him feel better, but I don't know how.

And it's much easier to be alone when I'm not really alone. Yes, I'll admit that sounds crazy. But solitude will do that to a person. Or a soul. Or whatever I am now.

I shouldn't have let his words earlier hurt me. Because he's right. Even if they could find a way to bring me back, where would I go? My body is gone. It's not like they can kill someone and give me her body. That is creepy and ridiculous, in equal parts.

Maybe a peaceful moving on is all I can hope for. That's even more reason to let them go. How badly will they hurt when I leave? If it's half as bad as I'm hurting right now at the thought of losing them, I can't put them through that. They already mean too much for me to destroy their hearts that way.

Did I just admit that I'm in love with these three? Maybe, but since I'm the only one who knows, I think it'll be okay. If I can move on before they get too attached, that will be better for them. But what if they're already too attached?

I can't let myself think that way. There is no way this can end that isn't heartbreak. If I could cry, I would be sobbing. I lay my head on Jack's shoulder, even though he can't feel me and doesn't know I'm here. I need the comfort he can give me right now. I wish I could feel his arms around me.

But then you risk him getting too close. Yeah, that's the real issue here. I spend the rest of the day in Jack's room because there's less chance of running into Spence or Murr here. The room smells like Jack's spicy, slightly woodsy cologne, and it calms me.

⁂

SPENCER

I understand why Kendall bolted, but that doesn't stop the ache in my chest. This situation feels impossible, but that doesn't mean we should give up. I want to embrace my time with her, even if it ends in the destruction of my heart. I'm already in love with her, and I don't care who knows it.

And the sex? Fan-fucking-tastic. I never expected to join the *I-fucked-a-ghost* club, but I'm not even put off by the thought. I spent so long pushing my gifts away, and the moment I met Kendall, all I've wanted was to expand them even more.

I want to be able to touch her without the ring. To be wherever she is. *Wait, am I saying I would die to be with her? Is that even possible?* Logistics be damned, I would do it if I knew that I'd be with her. That I could touch her, kiss her rosy lips, feel her arms wrapped around me.

Hmm. This is not where I thought my mind would be today. Maybe I should have taken Mom up on her offer to pay for therapy. As long as I don't actually hurt myself, I think I'll be okay. But I make a mental note to keep an eye on my urges, and call someone if things start to get out of hand. I'm not suicidal, and I don't want to be.

I'm just so obsessed with Kendall that I'm worried I may do something crazy without thinking it through. That idea makes me wonder about the guys. We should probably talk about this and keep an eye on each other. If I'm feeling this out of control, maybe they are too.

I tap on Jack's door, easing it open until I see that Kendall is lying on the bed next to him. Her eyes meet mine and I hold up my hand with the ring. She shakes her head, and I understand that she needs to be alone without being alone. Jack doesn't stir, so he must have fallen asleep. I close the door silently and head to find Murr.

CHAPTER FIVE

BREAKTHROUGH

KENDALL

THE GUYS HAVE BEEN working on their research for a couple of weeks now, and I've moved on from the hurt Jack's words caused me. He keeps trying to apologize, and I shut him down. There's no reason to say sorry for telling the truth.

"Fine, but I'd still like to try and make it up to you," he insists. It's his day with the ring, and as much as I've tried to pull back from them, I just can't.

"How do you plan to do that?" I ask, wondering if he's trying to get me out of my clothes. As far as I know, Spence hasn't told the other two about our, um, experience.

"A date," he answers with a devilish grin.

"Jack, you know I can't leave the property. And even if I could, people would think you're crazy—talking to yourself and all," I insist.

"Which is why our date is here at the house," he replies smoothly. He seems to have considered every objection I could make and has a counter to them all.

"Okay," I laugh. "But you know I can't exactly change clothes, right? I hope what I'm wearing is suitable."

He pulls me into his arms and hugs me. "You're perfect."

When he lets go, I give in to my impulse, grabbing his face in my hands and dragging it to me. His lips are soft and pliant against mine. Jack seems genuinely surprised by my actions, and I love it. His arms wrap around me again, tugging me closer, until I can feel what this kiss does to him.

It's such a power trip to know how badly these three want me. Jack is the least vocal, though, so it's harder to know what he's thinking. And he's been in his head lately about the turn their research took. Murr and Spence are out of the house today, hunting down a lead. They may have found a clairvoyant who knows something about the ring and how it works.

I still don't think it matters, but if it makes them feel better to try, I'll support it. And who knows? Maybe I'm wrong and they'll find a way to bring me back. All I really know is that I'm too far gone to push them away, no matter how badly this is going to end.

"That's enough of that for now. Otherwise, we'll never get to our date." Jack scolds me while I barely hold back a laugh.

I'm not sure that he'd be too upset about missing our date, but I don't say that.

❦

MURRAY

Spence and I walk into the tiny storefront, unsure of what to expect. When the door closes, a bell chimes. "I'll be right with you," a voice calls from the back.

When a figure emerges from behind the curtain in the back of the room, I feel Spence tense beside me, and I instinctively take a step backward. "Now, now, dearies, don't be afraid. Mama Nora won't hurt you," she says. As she walks toward us, I can see that she's an older woman with streaks of gray in her dark hair.

The dress she wears is tight, leaving little to the imagination. Mama Nora is a well-endowed grandmotherly type, with a gaze that seems to see everything at once. I guess that's a good thing for someone who claims to be clairvoyant.

My roommate and I exchange glances before he nudges me forward. I'll have to ask him later what he sees, since something has him on edge. I step forward cautiously and hold out my hand. "It's lovely to meet you, Mama Nora. We spoke on the phone. I'm Murray Cairns and this is my friend, Spencer Richardson. We're here about *Devoted Tempest*."

Her eyes go wide at the mention of the ring, even though we've already discussed it when I called. "I thought that was a joke," she admits, shaking my hand. "You know that thing is cursed, right? Y'all don't wanna be messing with cursed items. Trust me."

"With all due respect, Mama Nora, we understand your concerns, but we'd still appreciate it if you'd share any information you have about the ring with us," Spence says. He's still avoiding eye contact with the woman, but at least he's got my back here.

✦ ✦ ✦

SPENCER

As soon as I hear the voice from the back room, I know exactly who we've come to see. I can't tell Murr that I know Mama Nora, nor can I share *how* I know her. It would put my family in danger. I need to tell him that she can't be trusted. We have to avoid making a deal with her at all costs.

"Any information I give you will have to be a trade," she says in her syrupy-sweet voice. I'm certain from the gleam in her eyes that she recognizes me, too. I shake my head. *Not again, lady.*

"No deal. We don't have anything you want," I insist before Murr can agree to her terms. He looks at me and I shake my head.

"Not even a favor?" she asks. Murr looks at me pleadingly. There has to be another way to get this information. Someone else has to know how to control the ring's power.

"No. We're not trading anything. You can either tell us what you know about the ring, or we can leave," I say, holding up a hand when Murr starts to protest. I need to get him out of here before this goes bad. "On second thought, we'll just go somewhere else for the information. Thank you, and we're sorry for wasting your time."

I grab Murr's arm and drag him out of the storefront. As soon as the door clicks closed behind us, he whirls on me. "What the fuck was that about? You just cost us a week's worth of research. The least you can do is tell me why," he insists.

"Not here," I answer, walking away. I don't turn toward home, instead heading in the direction of the park. If we're having this conversation, it will be where I know we're not being spied on. Murr follows, cursing under his breath.

I hope Jack's plan to make up with Kendall is going better than our research. But I can't focus on that right now. I need to decide exactly how much I can tell Murr without giving away something that goes against our deal with Mama Nora.

I drop onto a bench in the middle of the park, where I can see all around us. The park isn't empty, but it's not too busy right now, either. Murr rolls his eyes at me as he sits down. I can tell that he notices my paranoid behavior, but I don't care. If he knew what I did about Mama Nora, he'd be paranoid too.

"Talk, or I'm going back there and listening to her offer," he says, crossing his arms over his chest.

I glance around one more time to be sure no one is listening. "Look, what I'm about to tell you can't go any further than this. It could cost lives. I need you to promise me." I lock eyes with him, and he stares back at me with a skeptical furrow of his brow.

"Sounds kinda cloak and dagger, doesn't it?" When I don't respond, he says, "Fine, I won't tell anyone what you tell me here. I don't understand how it could be that bad, though."

"You will. Trust me," I start. "Mama Nora is not just a psychic. She's a powerful witch. Don't ask me how I know, because that's part of the story I'm not allowed to share. She's dangerous. Anyone who's ever made a deal with her has lost something important to them. I can't take the chance that she'd take someone else I care about."

"Wait, you mean you've made a deal with her before?" he asks, leaning toward me and lowering his voice.

"Not me personally, but yeah. The deal was for me, and it nearly wrecked my family." I pause for a moment, trying to figure out how to explain it, then decide to just spit it out. "My psychic ability, the one I have now, is a side effect of the deal with her. When my parents went to Mama Nora, she promised to take my abilities away completely. And she did, for a very short period of time. I'm not sure if you realize how difficult it is for a kid to understand the difference between spirits and the living when they all look exactly the same."

Murr's eyes go wide. "You've never talked about your ability before."

"There's a reason for that. When I was young, before we met Mama Nora, I couldn't tell who was alive and who was a ghost. They all looked the same. I could interact with them exactly the same—we could talk, touch, everything. By the time I started school, people had begun to talk. Rumors that I was crazy went through the community like wildfire. It got to a point where parents wouldn't let me play with their kids, and no one in the community would even speak to me." I cover my face with my hands.

"It got so bad, when I was eight, I considered taking my own life. I just wanted it all to stop. So, my parents stepped in. They found Mama Nora and we went to see her. While we were there, I had a bad feeling in the pit of my stomach that something was off about this woman. My parents wouldn't listen. After all, what choice did we have? My father took the deal she offered, and she took my gift away," I explain.

"So, what happened?" Murr asks. "It's obvious that you still have abilities."

"That was an unfortunate complication. Before my father could keep his end of the bargain and do the favor Mama Nora requested, he was hit by a car and killed. I'm still not convinced that she wasn't responsible for his accident. She was so hateful when my mom and I went to explain the situation to her. Dad had every intention of keeping his end, but she didn't care. No one else could do it, so she decided to give part of what she took back," I say.

"Wow, man, that's rough. I understand why you stopped me from making a deal with her. But how will we get that information now?" he asks.

"I don't know yet," I admit. "But we have to find someone else. We can't make a bargain with her. I can't lose someone else I care about."

KENDALL

Jack leads me up to the attic. As he flips the switch to turn on the light, I gasp. "When did you guys come up here and do this?" I ask, turning in a circle to inspect the room.

What used to be dust and boxes is a fully furnished sitting room. "We took turns cleaning and moving stuff while you were occupied. I owe the guys big time for helping me with this. There was no way I could have done it without them."

"This is amazing," I say.

"We figured that this would give us a space to have dates with you, and have some privacy, without having to be in our bedrooms. As badly as we want you—and trust me, we do—we also want to spend time with you. I'll admit, I pushed for this because I wanted to make it up to you. I was an ass, and I'm very sorry," he says, pulling me into his arms.

"Oh, Jack," I sigh, pressing my lips to his for a quick kiss. "I told you; I overreacted. You didn't do anything wrong, and there was no reason for you to apologize."

He shakes his head. "I disagree. And the guys are on my side, so you'll just have to accept my apology. Otherwise, I'll be forced to find something bigger to do."

CHAPTER SIX

SETBACKS

JACKSON

Since we met Kendall, we've learned a lot about ghosts, or whatever she is now. Even when one of us has the ring on and can touch her, she doesn't eat or drink. But that doesn't stop us from finding interesting ways for her to experience things.

For example, this date I've prepared for her. I have chocolate covered strawberries and champagne. She can't directly ingest any of it, but when I eat one of the strawberries, then kiss her, she moans at the sweet and tart flavors.

"Jack, that's amazing. How did you figure that out?" she marvels at my idea.

I shrug. "Just a guess. Maybe me being a little selfish, too."

"How so?" She scrunches up her nose, not realizing what I've done here.

"It gets you to kiss me more," I laugh.

Her eyes go wide and for a minute, I think I've gone too far. She isn't amused, and she's going to walk away from me. Then I see it. The slightest hint of a smile crosses her lips. I watch as she tries to hold back the laugh that wants to escape. She tries to pretend that she's upset with me, but after a minute, she loses the battle and doubles over with laughter.

"I see. Well, it's a good plan," she admits, pulling me close and pressing her lips to mine. It starts as a chaste kiss, then deepens. Kendall wraps her arms around my neck as I drag her onto my lap.

KENDALL

Jack's date idea is sweet, and the fact that he found a way for me to enjoy strawberries again makes me giddy. When he pulls me onto his lap, I straddle him, wrapping my arms around his neck and pressing myself against him.

I grind against his growing erection as we make out. something about these men makes me wild. Maybe it's because I don't have a lot of experience, or maybe it's because they encourage me to try new things. All I know is that I'm obsessed and can't walk away.

"Kendall?" Jack breathes when I lean back slightly.

"Yes?" I stare into his eyes, memorizing the mocha with caramel streaks.

"I'm falling in love with you," he admits.

My eyes go wide. I had suspected that all three of them feel the same way I do, but none of us has said anything until now.

"Are you sure?" I ask, wanting to tell him how I feel, but suddenly overcome with fear.

He slides his hand into my hair, cupping the back of my head and pulling me closer. His lips barely brush against mine as he responds, "Positive."

"Oh, Jack," I sigh. "I feel it too. I'm just worried about how this would work. What if I stay this way?"

"Then we'll deal with it," he answers, kissing my neck. I thread my fingers through his short blond hair, holding him to me and tilting my head to give him better access. His lips on my skin feels so good; I don't want him to stop.

His teeth graze my flesh, and I shiver. I slide my hands down his shoulders then dig my fingers into his back. Jack groans, and I use that little bit of space between us to pull his shirt over his head, tossing it aside.

"That's not fair. Now you're wearing more clothes than I am. We'll have to fix that," he says, tugging at my shirt. I let him take it, blushing as he tosses it aside with his. "Much better."

He kisses me, dipping his tongue between my lips to stroke mine. Before I can tell him what I want, he breaks the kiss, pushing me back a little so I meet his gaze.

"I want you, Kendall. So, if this isn't something you're into, you have to tell me to stop. Otherwise, I'm going to bury myself in you and fuck you until you can't walk straight," he rasps.

I smirk. "I'd like to see you try," I answer. Another groan escapes him, and he flips us around on the blanket he has spread on the floor so that we're lying beside each other.

Jack runs his hands down my back, stopping briefly to unfasten my bra. He leaves it for a minute, stroking the skin along my spine before he finally throws my bra in the general direction of our other discarded clothes. Jack trails kisses down my neck to my chest, captures a nipple in his mouth, then bites down on it.

I arch my back and gasp in surprise. I wouldn't have expected that to feel as good as it does. I drag my nails along his back. "Jack," I say, urging him on.

While his mouth distracts me, he carefully strips off my clothes. Once I'm bared to him, his hands are everywhere, touching, stroking, caressing. It's as if he can't get enough of me, and I feel the same about him.

He shifts lower, and I growl. "I want to touch you."

Jack shakes his head. "I want to taste you." He spreads my legs open and settles between them, staring up at me. "Remember, if you want this to stop, you just have to say so." It's touching that he's concerned with what I want and am comfortable with, even as I can see his restraint wavering.

"Please," I beg, arching my hips toward his face. I want everything he can give me, and I'm tired of waiting.

That one word is all he needs. Jack descends on me like a starved man having his last meal. He kisses my pussy, licking along my seam, before sucking my clit into his mouth and swirling his tongue around it. My back arches and I cry out. I can't believe that he already has me on the edge of bliss. When he slides two fingers inside me, flicking my clit with his tongue, I scream with my release.

"Jack, I need you inside me," I pant, tugging at his shoulders to drag him up my body. He grins at me, letting me pull him up until our lips meet.

"I'll give you anything you want," he declares, wrapping his arms around me and kissing me hard. The taste of my pleasure mixed with him is almost too much for me.

Jack shifts our positions, notching himself at my entrance and pausing. "I've dreamed of this moment, Kendall." And with that, Jack slides his cock into me so slowly that I think I'm going to die a second time.

"Stop teasing me and fuck me already," I whine. Jack laughs and shakes his head, not bothering to speed up what he's doing.

Once he's fully seated inside me, he meets my gaze. "You feel so good." Before I can respond, he pulls almost all the way out of me and slams his dick back in, slapping his balls on my ass. His pace is fast and hard now, pushing me toward another release.

He thrusts into me, over and over, his pace erratic. I can tell he's chasing our pleasure while he tries to hold back. "Kendall," he pants. "I want to see you touch yourself." The simple request sends chills over my body. I rake my hands up my stomach, cupping my breasts and pinching the nipples. Jack groans. I slide one hand lower, rubbing a finger over my clit, sending shockwaves of pleasure through me.

"I'm gonna come," he says next to my ear, and his voice sends me over the edge. My walls contract, squeezing his cock and dragging the orgasm out of him. He collapses on top of me, then flips us over so I'm laying on his chest. "That was amazing," he says, holding me against him.

"It was," I agree, brushing my hair out of my face. We stay like that until the front door closes hard.

"Spence and Murr must be back. We should get dressed and see what they've found out," Jack says, rubbing a hand up my back. He pulls me down for a hard kiss, then eases me off him so he can sit up.

As soon as we're dressed, Jack and I walk down the stairs to find the guys.

⚜

MURRAY

The moment Jack comes into the living room, I feel Kendall's energy following him. It's his day with the ring, so I can't see our beautiful girl. I can sense that she's happy, though, and that makes me smile.

"Good, you're both here. We need to talk about some things," I say, gesturing to the couch for Jack to sit. From the way he positions himself, I can tell that Kendall is sitting on his lap. Damn, what I wouldn't give to see that.

I'm anxious to figure out this situation so that we can all see Kendall all the time; so we can kiss her, and show her our love without depending on a trinket we have to share.

"What's going on? Did you talk to that psychic?" Jack asks.

I glance at Spence, who is clenching his jaw. "Yes and no. She was a dead end. If she has any information, it will cost us too much to get it from her."

"What do you mean, it will cost us?" Jack asks, and it seems like he might be repeating something Kendall is asking.

"I mean, Spence knew her, and she's dangerous. We can't make a deal with her, so, we didn't get the information."

Jack looks at Spence, and I wonder for a minute if he's gonna ask about his story. I can tell Spence doesn't want to talk about it, so I keep talking. "We'll just have to find another way to figure out how to control the ring. I know it's not easy to play the waiting game, but what choice do we have?"

KENDALL

I listen as Murr explains that they couldn't get anything from the woman they went to see. I can't help wondering if this was the woman responsible for Spence's dad's death. He keeps his eyes averted when I look at him, though.

"Spence don't shut me out," I whisper, not wanting to interrupt what Murr is telling Jack.

He finally brings his eyes to meet mine, and the sorrow on his face is heartbreaking. Spence shakes his head and returns his gaze to the floor. When Murr pauses in his story, I look at Jack.

"Spence needs me right now," I say. Jack nods, slipping the dark metal ring from his finger and holding it out to Spence.

"Please take it, and we can go upstairs to talk while Murr finishes filling Jack in," I say, staring at Spence. He does as I ask, slipping the ring on as he stomps upstairs. I follow him to his room, not surprised when he slams the door.

"I don't want to talk about it," he says, turning away from me.

"Then don't talk. Just let me hold you," I answer, wrapping my arms around him from behind. He threads his fingers through mine and stands there for a minute, letting me comfort him. "It was her, wasn't it?" I ask. He nods in response, and I move to stand in front of him.

Without another word, I pull him into my arms, and we fall onto his bed together. I kiss his forehead and hold him, easing his head down on my chest. I hold him like that until he falls asleep. My fingers stroke his dark curls gently as Spence rests on me. I hate the pain I can still see in his face. He's been through so much.

If only there was something I could do to make this better for him. But I can't raise the dead, and I have no idea how to get revenge on this woman, since I can't leave this place. I'm stuck here, and all I can do is offer a little bit of comfort.

CHAPTER SEVEN

THE WITCH

KENDALL

AFTER A FEW DAYS of brooding, Spence finally tells me everything. Once he finishes his story, I disappear, trying desperately to find a way to get off this property and take that bitch down. Mama Nora deserves to be tortured for what she did to my sweet Spence and his family.

But every time I step off the front porch; every time I walk through the fence in the back; every time I walk through either of the neighbors' yards—I rematerialize in my old room that is currently occupied by Jackson. It's a little awkward for me, popping into the room when a man is stroking himself, but luckily it hasn't happened while he had the ring. So, he doesn't know it's happened.

Defeated, I sit on the front porch step, watching the world pass by. Yes, I'm being dramatic. I'm sure the guys will distract me from this melancholy angst I'm feeling soon. Until then, I'm going to sit here and pout.

The street isn't busy this time of day, but a few cars drive past. A couple of people walk by the house, and I wonder if they can sense me, because they stop talking as they walk in front of me. A few minutes later, I get the sensation that I'm being watched. I stand up and look around, certain that either Spence or Murr must be out here, since Spence can see me all the time, and it's Murr's day with the ring.

When my eyes meet a dark pair from across the street, a shiver goes through me. The elderly woman is heavy set, with dark hair that has streaks of gray in it. Even without Spence's description, I would have known in my soul that this is Mama Nora.

Her dark eyes lock onto mine, and somehow, I know that she can see me. It doesn't matter how she can do it. The issue is that now she knows where I am, and I know I can't escape. I have no idea what makes me feel like I'm in danger; hell, I'm dead—what more could she do to me at this point?

That question is less comforting than it should be. Holding her gaze, I dematerialize, relocating myself to Jack's room before searching the house for Spence and Murr. They can get Jack and then we can talk about this.

"Spence! Murr!" I shout, hoping that they'll hear me. I find them in the living room. Relief washes over me when Jack is with them. "We have a problem," I say.

Jack looks at the guys, understanding that something is happening. "What is it?"

"Kendall just popped in. She looks scared. Something is wrong," Spence tells him.

I hate that I can't talk to all three of them right now. But I guess I should be relieved that they tell each other nearly everything. "The witch is outside," I say, gesturing toward the front of the house. "And she can see me. I swear, she was staring right into my eyes. Then a creepy grin spread across her face, and I made myself scarce."

"So, she knows where we live," Spence says with a shiver. "That's not good."

"What can she do, though?" Murr asks.

"I don't know, but her staring at me made me feel uneasy. She scares me," I admit. The guys relay what I'm saying to Jack.

"Can she even do anything to Kendall, though? Like, what could she do to a ghost?" Jack asks. I can tell he's not joking around. He really has no idea. Honestly, I don't either, but I don't want to find out.

"It's better if we don't know," Spence says. "She's powerful and has abilities that I don't know anything about. She's dangerous. We need to stay away from her."

"But that will be nearly impossible now that she knows where we live. And since she seemed pretty desperate to convince us to make a deal," Murr says.

We've rehashed their encounter with the witch so many times since Spence finally opened up to me. I don't know what we can do to protect ourselves. Especially if he's right and Mama Nora is the one who killed his dad.

"We can't do anything other than keep doing what we've been doing," Jack interjects.

"Sadly, I think Jack is right. I mean, you guys can try to avoid her, but I can't leave this property. If she comes after me, I have no way to get out," I say. "I don't want to think about it, but worst case, you guys need to leave town."

As soon as Murr tells Jack what I said, he flips out. "We're not leaving. The four of us are a unit. We will figure this out together. I'm not letting some random crazy woman chase us off." He's still not convinced that magic is real, or that Mama Nora could actually be a witch.

I kinda wish I felt the way he does about the supernatural. But I've seen too much, even before I died, to think that magic is imaginary. I know it's real. And sometimes it's scary.

"I just want you guys to be safe. No matter what that costs me. Please, promise me that if she comes here, you'll run. Don't try to face off with her," I beg them.

Spence repeats my words to Jack, and he shakes his head. "No chance."

Murr and Spence agree with him. "We're not going any-where."

"And we're certainly not leaving you to deal with the witch on your own."

SPENCER

No matter how many times Kendall begs us to leave, we're not doing it. I don't know exactly what Mama Nora wants, but I plan to find out. Even if that means facing the evil witch again. It's not like she can force me to do anything if I don't accept her offer. Sure, she could kill me, but I don't think that's what she wants.

There's something else going on here, and I have to know what it is. Somehow, the ring, and Kendall, are related to my father's death. If I can't figure out how, I may lose more than I already have.

Standing in front of the tiny storefront once again, I find myself wishing I hadn't decided to come alone. What if this crazy witch locks me away and I never see Kendall again? No, that's not going to happen. I won't let it. I have to be stronger than she is.

I take a deep breath, then walk through the door. Part of me wants to stop the bell from chiming and announcing my arrival. But I don't. I want her to know I'm here. I need to talk to her.

"I'll be right there, dearie. I'm glad to see you've come alone this time," she calls. A shiver races up my spine at her words, and I'm certain that she knows it's me in her shop, even though she shouldn't be able to see me. Maybe she has hidden cameras around the store. I shake my head to push that thought away. Mama Nora does not need cameras to see what's going on. She has too much power for that to be an issue.

I don't bother to respond, glancing around the shop as I wait for her to join me.

"You know, I wondered how much time would pass before you came to see me. I'm sure you have questions. I'll be happy to provide answers—for a price," she says, pushing the curtain open and walking out into the storefront.

"I'm not making a deal with you. No matter what you say, I know that you killed my father. I don't know why, or what you want with Kendall, but I will not make any deals with you," I insist.

"Oh, dearie, you won't have a choice. You will make a deal with me. But we'll get to that later. For now, I'm feeling a little nostalgic. Let's chat. You may ask me your questions, and I'll give you some answers." Before I can tell her to go to Hell, she holds up a hand. "At no charge this time, dearie, since I feel as if I owe you. But I'm only giving you three questions for free. Understood? If you want more information than that, you'll have to make a trade."

The old woman's voice grates against me, reminding me of when my parents brought me to her for help. We'd thought she was the answer to our problems. Instead, she destroyed our lives.

"Fine. Three questions that you have to answer honestly." I pause, and she nods. I take that for agreement and continue. "I'll need a moment to gather my thoughts," I respond. She nods, busying herself with straightening up a tray of crystals and a display of tarot cards while I consider. With only three questions, I'm not sure what's the most important to ask.

"I'm ready," I say, deciding that I'm just going to wing it and hope for the best.

"Remember, only three questions for free," she reminds me as she takes a seat at a small table, gesturing for me to sit across from her.

I take the seat, forcing my face to remain neutral. "Why did you kill my father?"

"Oh, child. That is a very long, very boring story. A story that won't change any of the events that have transpired. I will tell you that everything I've done has been for a singular purpose. Your father's death brought us closer to my goal. And as angry as you are about it, he gave his life freely as payment for my services," she explains calmly.

Why would my father agree to give his life to this woman? Surely, she's lying. This can't be true. "We're done here. I can't believe anything you say, so there's no point in asking any further questions," I say, standing up to leave.

"Wait," she insists, pulling out a sealed envelope and handing it to me. "If you don't believe me, perhaps you will believe your father's words."

I stop myself from asking what the fuck she's talking about, because I sense that she wants me to waste my final questions. All of this is a ruse to pressure me into some ridiculous bargain. I will not fall for it. Turning the envelope over in my hand, I'm certain that the writing is my father's.

Am I ready to open this and read it? Not even a little. But what choice do I have? I peel the flap open and pull out a sheet of paper, written in my father's hand.

My son,

I don't expect you to understand what's happened. I only hope that Mama Nora is able to take your affliction away, so that you may have the best life possible.

I couldn't tell you or your mother the cost for the witch's services. No price is too high to protect those I love.

I made my decision out of love, not necessity. We could have continued without her assistance, but your life would have been miserable. I can't stand by and let you suffer when there's something I can do about it.

Please forgive me,
Dad

The simple note gives so little explanation but is totally my father. There's no way that he didn't write it. I don't understand why the witch bargained for his life, though. Should I ask? No. There are more pressing issues to handle.

"Thank you. That bit of closure does help. I have two questions left," I say, holding back the emotion that threatens to overwhelm me. I have to keep this conversation on track; we need answers.

The old woman nods at me, a sly smile crossing her features. "You do indeed. What else would you like to know?"

Too much to fit into two questions, but I won't say that. She'll just use it to push me into some shady deal. "How is Kendall's death related to my father's?"

Mama Nora's sly smile turns cold. "I thought you wanted to know more about your father and his deal. I hadn't realized you'd ask about the girl."

"You said three questions. There were no other parameters. I am free to ask whatever three questions I want you to answer. My first question was about my father's death. You answered that one satisfactorily, for the most part. My second question is about the relationship of the two deaths. I expect an honest answer," I snap. Keeping my focus is difficult, but I can't let her get under my skin. I have to ask my questions or we'll never get answers.

I watch as she mulls over her answer before she speaks. "I do not wish to answer this question. Ask a different one," she says.

Shaking my head, I respond, "No. You will answer *this* question. That was the offer. Three questions; three honest answers. So, tell me, *what does Kendall's death have to do with my father's death?* You must answer my question."

CHAPTER EIGHT

GETTING ANSWERS

JACKSON

ARGUING ABOUT SOME CRAZY woman who thinks she's a witch gets old fast. I don't want to admit to anyone, least of all the three people I live with, that I'm starting to believe in magic and the paranormal. It's hard to argue against it when you're in love with a ghost. I decide to do some research on my own and see what I can find out about this witch who may be after my loved ones.

Is it bad that I feel less anxious sharing my secret belief with Mrs. Ward, the librarian, than with my chosen family? I try not to think about it too much as I walk into the library. The sweet older woman has a few books set aside for me, and I plan to read through them here instead of taking them home. If I find something useful, then I'll approach the subject with the others.

KENDALL

Jack and Spence are both gone today, leaving me alone with Murr. The past few weeks have been rough for everyone, and I know that he's worried about all of it. While there is a lot to figure out, I'm not as worried as I was before.

He's trying to distract me with a movie, but I'm not really interested in that right now. So, I've made it my mission to distract him from it. There are a few ways I can accomplish this, but I think I'm gonna go the naughty route.

I start by resting my hand on his thigh, just above his knee. When that doesn't seem to faze him, I lay my head on his shoulder. No obvious reaction; I guess I'll have to up my game. It's not like I have a lot of experience, but I should be able to seduce Murr, right? It's almost easier to be intimate with Spence or Jack; they're not hesitant to show me that they want me. Murr is more reserved. It's like he's scared that he'll chase me off.

I have to find ways to convince him that isn't going to happen. Starting right now. I turn my face, tucking it toward his neck. His sharp intake of breath when my lips meet the tender skin just above his collar is all I need to nudge me on. While I nip and lick his neck, I slide my hand higher on his thigh.

"Kendall," he breathes.

"Mmhm," I answer against his skin.

"What are you doing? I thought we were watching a movie," he whispers.

"You're watching a movie. I'm busy," I say, not moving away. Murr tenses as I slide my hand further up his thigh, settling it right next to his hip as my lips continue to explore the tender skin of his neck.

"Kendall, you have to stop," he breathes.

"Why?" I ask. "Don't you like it?"

"That's exactly why. I like it too much, and I don't want to take advantage of you," he answers. Oh, this guy. He's too cute.

"Murr, come on. You're not going to take advantage of me. I'm the one instigating, here. If anything, I'm the one who will be taking advantage," I laugh.

He shakes his head, inching away from me. My eyes narrow and I lean the other direction, pulling my hand away. "Murr," I say, failing to keep the hurt from my voice. "Do you not want me?"

"What? That's ridiculous. Of course I want you. Kendall, it's not that, really. I just don't feel right taking things further when I haven't found a way to bring you back yet. Desire has nothing to do with it," he insists.

I can't help feeling rejected, though. I mean, I put myself out there, trying to give him my attention, and he stopped me. "Oh, okay." I have no other response.

"Let's just watch the movie, okay?" he asks.

I smile and nod, fighting back the tears that are only possible when I'm close to whoever wears the ring. I shift, turning away from him and toward the movie. It hurts all over again when he doesn't reach out for me or even try to touch me. I have no idea what I did to push him away. Until now, I thought that he'd wanted me as much as the other two did.

⁂

SPENCER

I wait for Mama Nora to answer my question, wondering if she's actually going to tell me anything helpful.

"Are you certain that's the question you want to ask?" And there it is. She's as much as admitted that she only offered answers because she thought she knew what I would ask.

"I'm certain. Now you can answer, or I can leave," I insist. Once again, she holds up a hand to stop me from leaving.

"There are things you don't yet understand, child. So much is connected, and it's impossible to give you only the answers you seek," she says. I can tell that she didn't want to tell me that much. Maybe if I keep pushing, I can get the answers we need.

"You were the one who offered to answer three questions at no charge. If you're not going to give me answers, I'm leaving, and I'll never be back. I'm sure I can find someone else who knows," I threaten. We both know that I need her for this. I have no idea where I would find someone with knowledge of what happened, since this deal was made between my father and this witch.

I know that Mama Nora wants something from me, but I haven't figured out yet what it is. And somehow, Kendall and my dad are connected to it. "I know you won't tell me every-thing. I can accept that. But I need to know how Kendall's death is related to my father's. I don't know how to help her, and you're the only chance we have for answers." I hate being even that honest with her, but I have no choice other than making a deal. And I won't do that.

The old witch stares at me for a long moment while she seems to be considering my admission. "Fine. I'll tell you what I can. But you aren't going to like it, and I don't think you'll believe half of it," she says.

I relax into my chair, giving her time to collect herself and start talking. She's right, I probably won't believe half of what she tells me. I don't trust her.

"Did your parents tell you where your power originates from?" she asks. I shake my head, and she continues, "I didn't think so. You'll have to ask your mother for that answer; it's the one thing I will not answer. As for your girl and your father, yes, their deaths are connected. The how of it is complicated, and I only know half the answer."

I glare at her when she pauses.

"I told you that your father gave his life as part of our bar-gain. That is true, but what I didn't tell you is that he sacrificed himself in a ceremony to remove your powers. I know that isn't the story you were told, and I'm sorry for the lies. Trust me, they have been a necessary part of this situation."

She pauses again, standing and walking to the back room. When she returns, she carries a tea tray. I shake my head when she offers me a cup but wait patiently as she pours her own tea and settles back in her seat.

"Since you've obviously been researching everything, you most likely already know that the ring, *Devoted Tempest*, was created by a witch with the help of a demon. What you don't know, is that I am the witch who created it. That ring was meant to take your powers, but something went wrong with your father's sacrifice. *Devoted Tempest* only absorbed half of your powers, leaving the other half inside of you. I haven't figured out how your girl ended up with my ring, but that is what killed her. I wasn't sure until I went to see her," Mama Nora explains.

"I need proof of your words," I insist, careful not to make it a question. I still have one thing I want to ask when she's finished with her tale.

"I understand your hesitation, but I can assure you, every word of it is true. Both are dead now because of that ring. There is no way to bring either one back," she argues.

Somehow, I know that she's right. My soul believes her, even if I don't want to. I almost ask if she's sure, then realize that's probably what she's hoping for. I can't waste my last question like that. I have to be careful.

"That's all I can tell you about their connection," she says, letting me know that she's finished with her story. I won't get anything else out of her on this. It's time to break out the last question—the one she definitely won't want to answer.

"Fine. For my last question…How do we control the ring's power?" I ask, even though there are a million other questions I have. I refuse to make a deal with this witch, even if I am fully certain that she's been honest with me tonight.

Her eyes go wide, and she stares at me. Her jaw works as she opens and closes her mouth. I wonder what's going through her mind right now.

"I, I can't," she stutters, her eyes going even wider with what looks like fear.

"You can't tell me how to control the ring, but you promised to answer three questions. That's my third question. Therefore, you have to answer," I insist.

Mama Nora closes her eyes as if she's saying a silent prayer. When her eyes open again, she locks hers with mine. "You don't know what you're asking, child. Please, choose any other question. Don't force this out of me."

"Tell me," I insist again. I can't explain what happens, but it feels as if I'm compelling the answer from her. The old witch fights against the words, even as they come out of her.

"You are the only one who can control it, since it's half of your power." As soon as the words are out of her mouth, she collapses on the floor. I'm not sure if she's even still breathing, but I don't stick around to find out.

CHAPTER NINE

WHAT NOW?

KENDALL

STILL REELING FROM MURR'S rejection, once the movie ends, I disappear for a while. I thought that he was interested, but maybe I misunderstood. Or maybe he's just weirded out by the idea of having sex with a ghost. That's probably more likely, but it still hurts like any rejection would.

When Spence gets home, he looks upset but shakes his head at me when I try to approach him. Great, another rejection. If I could leave this place, I would. But I'm stuck here, because my soul just won't move on. Once again, I find myself wishing I could form tears without being near the ring.

Since both the guys are in their rooms, I hide in the attic space that they turned into "my room" so I don't accidentally run into them. I think I just need some time away from them to sort out what I'm feeling. I hate this lonely, isolated feeling.

I can't stand feeling so helpless and abandoned. I'm sure that isn't what the guys intend, but it's where we are. With everything that's happened, I stop and ask myself why a lot. Why did this happen to me? I can't figure out what I did to cause this. Was it just bad luck? Or did I unknowingly piss someone off and they somehow killed me and cursed me to be stuck here?

I don't know how long I sit there, staring out the window at the back yard, wallowing in my misery. A light tapping on the door frame catches my attention, and I jerk my head toward it.

Jack stands there with a sad smile. "I got the ring from Murr. He said that you were upset with him, and he thought I might be able to help."

Mortification spreads across my face as Jack walks over to me. "Did he tell you exactly what happened?" I ask, not wanting any of these guys to think less of me.

He shrugs. "More or less. He didn't say why; just that he turned you down when you tried to get intimate with him. Personally, I think he's a little weirded out by the idea of having sex with a ghost. And with him being the one who can feel energies, that does seem strange. But maybe he's just not ready yet. We've all been so laser focused on figuring out how to bring you back and searching for answers. Give him some time, okay?"

I nod and Jack slides his arm around my shoulders, pulling me close to him. "It just felt like he wasn't interested, ya know? And this is kinda weird; talking to you about another guy."

Jack laughs, jostling me against him. "You have nothing to feel weird about. Murr, Spence, and I all feel connected to you. If you're into all of us, we'll find a way to share. This isn't about us. You are the most important thing."

His words are sweet, but I wonder if he really means them. It's not like I can be with all three of them at once. Damn, that would be hot, though. I let myself fall into that daydream for a moment, coming back to reality when Murr in my imagination turns me down much the same way Murr in real life did. I have two guys who want me, that should be enough, right

❧❀❀❀❀❧

MURRAY

I realize that I hurt Kendall's feelings, and I really didn't mean to. As much as I want to tell her the truth, I can't. It's mortifying that I don't know enough about sex to figure out what I'm supposed to do with her. And I'm not telling the guys either.

My lack of experience is my own problem. I'll figure it out at some point. I have to, right? But I'm definitely not going to walk up to any of them and admit that I'm a virgin and the idea of having sex freaks me out.

I handed the ring off to Jack as soon as he walked in, letting him think that I'm moving slow with Kendall because the ghost thing freaks me out. Honestly, her being a ghost has nothing to do with it. I just don't know how to tell her about my inexperience.

When he heads upstairs to talk to her, I nearly follow him. I hate that I hurt her, but I can't do anything to fix it right now. Researching sex isn't going to be easy. I'll have to find time when everyone else is asleep, or when I'm out of the house. With that and the cursed ring, balance will be hard to find.

The knock on my door catches me off guard. Is it Jack returning the ring, or has he come to yell at me for hurting Kendall? I open the door hesitantly, sighing out a breath when I see Spence standing there instead. "What's up?" I ask.

He stares at me blankly. "Can I borrow the ring for a bit? Or are you and Kendall busy?"

"Oh, um. I think I made her mad. So, I gave Jack the ring to talk to her. I think they're upstairs," I answer, twisting my hands. Maybe I should just tell him what happened and see if he can help me.

"Okay, I'll just wait," he says and turns to leave.

"Spence," I start, hesitating when he pins me with a stare. "Nevermind, it's nothing."

He nods and walks off. I need to find someone to talk to about this or come up with a way to research what I need to know without anyone finding out. I'm not sure which is the better option. I have to do something, though, because I can't keep hurting Kendall.

SPENCER

After my talk with Mama Nora, I head home and straight to my room. I probably shouldn't push Kendall away right now, but she looks as upset as I feel. I can't deal with that right now. I need to figure out what the old witch meant when she said I was the only one who could control the ring.

When I ask Murr for the ring, I can tell that something is bothering him, but I don't have time to placate him. I need to figure out how to control the ring, and what Kendall's death has to do with my father's. I'm more annoyed with myself than the crazy old woman.

I knew that she wouldn't actually answer my questions, even though she offered to. Especially since she made it clear that she wants a bargain from me. What does she want?

Since I can't get the ring at the moment, and I have no other way of obtaining answers, I decide to call my mom. There's no way she knows anything about what the witch told me, though, so I don't expect to learn anything new.

I dial and wait while it rings. "Spencer? Is everything okay, son?" My mother's voice is warm but laced with concern.

"I'm fine, Ma. There's just something I need to ask you. But before that, how are you?" I don't know how she's going to react to my questions, but I won't let that stop me from asking.

She tells me about her week and a disagreement with one of her neighbors about them leaving shoes in the hallway. Then she turns the conversation around on me. "But none of that is why you called me. What's wrong?"

Unable to lie to her, I quickly explain the situation, including Kendall's predicament, the ring's strange involvement, and the witch. "She said that Dad sacrificed his life to take my power, but that it didn't work. Do you know anything about that?"

"Spencer, I don't think you should be messing with that woman. She's insane. Please tell me that you didn't make a deal with her," Ma says.

I shake my head, even though she can't see me. "No, Ma, I didn't make a deal with her. I made it very clear to her that I won't be making any deals with her, and neither will any of my friends. But she said things, and I don't know if I can believe her."

"What kind of things?" I can hear the fear in Ma's voice, and it makes me hesitate. Maybe I shouldn't tell her. But there's no other way I'll get answers if I don't.

"She said that she created the ring, Ma. With a demon's help. She didn't come right out and say it, but she seemed to be implying that Dad was a demon. That's insane, right? It's not possible," I insist. I don't know if I'm trying to convince myself or my mom.

Ma sighs before she answers. "Spencer, there are things you don't know about your father. I promised him I wouldn't tell you. Please, son, leave this alone. It won't end the way you want."

"Ma, what do you mean? I need answers. I have to help Kendall. You can't ask me to leave her," I argue, my anger building. Why is she trying to hide things from me?

"Son, that witch is dangerous, and there's nothing you can do to save the girl if she's already dead," Ma says. Her matter-of-fact tone is pissing me off.

"Look, Ma, I understand that you're worried. Yes, Mama Nora is dangerous. But I'm not backing down. Would you rather I try to do this without all the relevant information? Because you know I'm not going to let this go. Please. I'm asking you to help me." I'm not planning to beg, but I'm not above it.

I can't let Kendall suffer because of something my father got involved in before we ever even knew her. It's not right; and I was raised better.

Another sigh echoes through the phone. "You are so much like him. I shouldn't be surprised. Fine, but you're not going to like it. And I don't know everything. Your father didn't want me to be a target, so he kept some of it to himself. I'll tell you what I can."

"I'm listening," I say, pausing to let her tell the story.

"You've heard the story of how your father and I met. That adorable coffee shop meet cute story was just that, though. A story. In reality, we met when I accidentally summoned him to my dorm room one night."

"What?" I ask, confusion gripping me.

"Your father was a demon, Spencer. But our love story was exactly what we always shared with you, except for how we met. We fell in love and had you. I was terrified that you would have powers like him, and when you demonstrated your gifts, I freaked out. Your father found Mama Nora and convinced her to help us strip your powers.

"We didn't realize at the time that she was going to try to trap your powers in that ring. I don't know what she intended to use it for, but there are rumors and stories about it. I argued with him for days about it, begging him not to go through with it. The only way to take your powers was for him to sacrifice his life."

"Ma, are you serious?" Everything the witch told me is true. My legs give out and I drop to the floor. I can't process any of this right now.

"Spencer, please. I need to get it all out. When the spell or ceremony or whatever didn't take all of your powers, that evil woman tried to come after you again. I managed to find a shaman to protect you, but now that you're an adult, you're on your own. Please, promise me that you won't make any deals with her."

CHAPTER TEN

SECRETS COME OUT

JACKSON

SPENCE IS ACTING WEIRD, and so is Murr. Neither one seems interested in hanging out with Kendall, and I'm starting to wonder what their problems are. When it's his turn with the ring, Spence takes it and leaves.

Since I had it a moment ago, I know that Kendall is standing to my left. I can't see or hear her, but I'm sure she's upset. I have to help her.

"I'll go after him," I say, dashing out the door just in time to see Spence turn the corner. It looks like he's going to the park.

I follow, not trying to hide the fact that I'm behind him. If he notices me, he doesn't make it obvious.

Two blocks later, he crosses the street and takes a left. By the time he stops just inside the border of the public park, I've managed to catch up to him. "Hey, Spence," I call, slowing from my jogging pace.

He turns and glares at me. "Why are you following me?"

"Kendall is upset, man. What are you doing?" I see no reason to pull punches with him.

"I'm trying to sort things out. I just need some space, okay?" he says, turning away from me.

"Why are you pushing everyone away? Between you and Murr, you've got Kendall convinced that there's something wrong with her. And honestly, I'm starting to think the two of you would rather not have me around, either." My words are cold, matching my tone completely. I want him to understand exactly how Kendall and I are feeling.

"It's not like that. I have to figure this out on my own. I can't let anyone else get hurt because of me," he says. For the first time since I caught up to him, I notice that his eyes are glimmering with unshed tears. He really does think he's protecting us by pushing us away.

"Spence, you can't do this on your own. We're a team. If you can't talk to Kendall about it, at least share with me. I understand you don't want to hurt her, but you are. I can't keep defending you when you act this way. Please, just sit down with me and tell me what's going on," I say. I hate the idea of begging, but I will if I have to. I can't let him keep secrets from the rest of us. We won't figure this out if we're disjointed. It's going to take teamwork to find answers.

"Fine, let's go sit over there," he says, gesturing to a bench on the other side of the park. I follow him, scared to let him get out of my sight. I'm not sure he's actually going to talk to me, and I don't want to lose him now.

⁕⁕⁕

KENDALL

Since Spence left with the ring, I'm alone. He's the only one who can see or hear me without the ring. My heart swelled when Jack chased after him. I know he did it for me. This whole situation is ridiculous, and I hate how much I've come to depend on these guys.

I can't help feeling like there's something wrong with me, since neither Spence nor Murr wants anything to do with me now. What did I do to mess this up? Jack insists that I didn't do anything, but I'm not sure I can believe him.

With Jack chasing after Spence, I know I'll get answers later. But why would Spence take the ring and run off with it? I stare out the window, considering possibilities. As I watch the world go by, I notice movement beside the fence in the back yard.

Leaning closer, I realize it's Mama Nora. She's looking for a way to get into the yard. Shit, I can't even warn Murr. As soon as I see her manage to open the gate, I search the house for Murr. He's relaxing in the living room. I rush over to him, wondering how I can get him to understand he's in danger.

His body tenses when I get close. I can tell that he senses me, even though he doesn't speak. Glancing around the room, I know that he's been watching TV and relaxing since the guys left. I don't blame him, but I wish there was some way to make him understand.

A soft snick echoes through the house, but Murr is oblivious to the noise. The back door swings open, and footfalls get closer. I try to grab Murr's hand and pull him in the opposite direction, but my hand slides right through his.

He pulls his hand to his chest and rubs it as if touching me hurt. A pang of regret and pain courses through me. I have no way to let him know what's happening or protect him from this witch.

I can't do anything but watch as Mama Nora creeps closer, smiling maniacally. "Murr! Get out of here! Go, now!" I yell at him. But he can't hear me. My screams are met with silence. My eyes lock on the woman who is now stalking one of the men I'm falling for. "You can't do this," I say quietly, unable to keep the waver of fear out of my voice.

The witch moves more quietly than I would expect. When she stands behind Murr, her eyes lock onto mine. Her evil grin spreads wider, and she looks even more psychotic than she did before. I hadn't noticed before that she's carrying a cane. But the moment she raises it to swing at Murr's head, it's all I can focus on.

The wooden cane, with what looks like a marble handle, comes down sharply, smacking against Murr's skull with a sickening crack. "Now you belong to me," the witch says with a laugh.

"I'll never belong to you," I answer, desperately trying to figure out what I can do to stop her from killing him.

SPENCER

I'm not thrilled that Jack followed me to the park, but I understand why he did it. He's feeling protective of Kendall, and I like that. It's not my intent to hurt her. I just have to figure this out so I can save her.

I've been trying to process everything my mom confirmed since our conversation. I'm a half-demon, and that's where my psychic abilities come from. It's obvious that Mama Nora didn't know enough about demons or half breeds when she tried to take my powers. That's why the ritual didn't work. I stare down at the ring on my finger. This small piece of metal holds half my power.

I should tell the others, but I can't. It all makes sense now—how wearing the ring allows people without powers to physically interact with ghosts. I don't know how I didn't make the connection before. Feeling stupid and foolish, I turn to face Jack as we sit on a bench in the park.

"Okay, man. I'm here, and I'm ready to listen. What is going on?" he asks.

As much as I want to avoid this conversation, I don't. Sitting on a bench in the park, I spill my biggest secrets to one of my best friends, praying like Hell that he won't decide he's done with me when I'm finished. Jack listens as I explain my story, including my father's demon lineage, his sacrifice, the ring; everything.

When I'm done, I brace for his reaction. I expect him to yell, to scream, to storm off in a huff. Instead, he sits there, quiet and withdrawn. "Jack?" I say, forcing him to look at me.

He nods, scrubbing his hands down his face. "I heard you. I'm not going anywhere. It's just a lot to process. I can see why you needed some time alone with it."

"You're not upset that I didn't tell you right away?" I ask, unable to hold the question back.

He shakes his head. "I understand. But you're gonna have to tell Kendall and Murr. We need to face this as a family. You can't just run off when you learn something upsetting. If we want to fix this and be with Kendall, we have to do it together."

I take a second to process his words. "You're right. It's not fair to anyone for me to lock things away. No matter how badly I want to handle this on my own, I can't. But what about Mama Nora's declaration that I'm the only one who can control the ring's power?"

"We'll figure it out together. If you're the only one who can wield it, then that's what we'll do. But you can't just make that decision for us. You have to let us in so we can help you. You're not alone here, even if you think you are," Jack insists.

"Thanks, Jack. That's exactly what I needed to hear. We should go back home and talk to Murr and Kendall, shouldn't we?" I know it's the right thing to do, even if it's going to be the most difficult thing I've ever dealt with. Jack nods, and we start toward home.

***

MURRAY

I wake up, feeling stiff and sore. My head is throbbing. When I try to rub it, I realize that my hands are tied behind me, and I'm chained to a chair. I blink a few times to clear my eyes. Then I shake my head, realizing quickly that was a bad idea. A wave of nausea overtakes me, and I swallow the bile that threatens to come up. Where am I?

Closing my eyes for a minute, I try to remember what I can from before everything went dark. I was watching TV when I sensed Kendall enter the room. Before I could even consider trying to communicate with her, a searing pain shot through my head and the world went black. Where the fuck am I?

I can see the outline of my phone in my pocket, and I wonder for a minute if I can make a call without touching it. I can't risk my captor taking it—that phone may be the only thing that can lead the guys to me.

"Hello?" I call tentatively, keeping my voice quiet. I wait a minute before calling out again, louder this time, "Is anyone there?" I hold my breath while I anticipate a response. Silence meets my ears once again, and I let my breath out slowly.

Giving my eyes time to adjust to the dim lighting here, I start looking around. There's nothing familiar to me here, so I'm pretty sure that I'm not still at home. It would be great if I'd just been locked in my own basement, right? That's too much to ask for. At least I would have had Kendall near me if that had been the case. Fear stabs through my heart. Kendall. She's alone at the house now, and there's no one to protect her.

I know she's dead, but that doesn't mean I don't still worry about her. I've been trying to figure out how to tell her about my inexperience but haven't gotten there yet. Now it looks like I may never get the chance to. Regret fills me until I'm fighting tears. I can't give up now. Leaving Kendall alone is not an option.

Leaning from side to side, I try to knock the chair over. When it falls on its side easily, I shout in surprise before grunting at the impact of landing on my side. The flimsy wood of the chair splinters and breaks, leaving me chained to a pile of rubbish. It takes some work to get the chains moved so I can stand up. My hands are sill tied behind my back, but I'm able to maneuver myself to get them in front of me.

Using my teeth, I fight with the rope that holds my hands together. After what feels like hours, I finally get part of it to loosen enough that I can free myself. I pull out my phone and check to see if I have signal.

Hiding in a dark corner of this room, I type out a quick text to Jack and Spence in our group chat.

Guys, I'm in trouble. Don't know what happened, no clue where I am. Help!

After hitting send, I wait for their response, debating if I should stay here or try to escape.

CHAPTER ELEVEN

DISASTERS

MURRAY

I WAIT LONGER THAN I want for a response. My heart is racing, thumping in time with the pain in my skull. I know I must have a concussion, because the world spins every time I move. I fight against the nausea as darkness tries to take me again. Fuck. I guess I took a harder hit to the head than I thought. I wish I could remember what happened.

I get a text reply from one or both of the guys. At this point, I can't see clearly enough to read it. I can't stay here. I have to at least try to escape. Standing, I brace myself against the wall as

I push through my blurred vision. I can't give up now. I don't want to die or abandon Kendall.

I'm pretty sure that I'm alone here, since I made a lot of noise breaking the chair and no one came down here. Holding myself up against the wall, I move toward the stairs. Climbing them is slow and painful, although I think my only injuries are to my head.

The door at the top of the stairs is unlocked, the handle turning easily in my hand. I open it slowly and peer out into an empty kitchen. After a moment, I step through the door and lean against it for support.

The back door calls to me from across the room, and I stumble toward it. My vision clears a little when I stop to catch my breath. I take a chance and look at my phone.

Murr, we're on our way. Hold on, we'll be there as soon as possible.

The room spins again and I close my eyes against the sensation. I can't stay here, even if the guys are on their way. The door opens easily when I finally manage to turn the knob. I make it outside into the back yard, leaning against the side of the house as I walk around it.

Everything goes dark, and I collapse, barely registering the arms that catch me before I hit the ground.

JACKSON

Spence and I catch Murr as he collapses. We exchange a look, lifting him and carrying our unconscious friend down the street. "I'm glad he wasn't further away," Spence grunts as we struggle to get our front door open.

Once we're inside, we take Murr to the couch. Spence hands me the ring so I can see and talk to Kendall, since he has that ability without it. She's frantic with worry over Murr.

"Oh, no! Is he okay? I tried so hard to stop that witch from hurting him, but I couldn't." Kendall paces the floor, her eyes locked on Murr the whole time.

"It's hard to tell with his injuries. He's barely breathing. We need to get his head cleaned up so we know what we're dealing with," Spence says.

I rush to the kitchen and grab towels, a bowl of hot water, and our first aid kit. Racing back to the living room, I hand the supplies to Spence, who starts cleaning up Murr's head and face.

"I need you to check him for broken bones. Especially his chest and ribs. I'm not sure if he has a collapsed lung, or if this head injury is just that bad," he orders. Immediately, I start running my hands over our friend, searching for broken bones.

"I'm not finding anything that feels out of place," I say, pausing to watch as Spence wipes blood from Murr's head. "It's not doing any good. He's still bleeding so much."

"I know. I'm worried that he's losing too much blood. We should call an ambulance," Spence insists. "This is worse than I thought."

KENDALL

I feel helpless as the EMTs follow Jack into the living room and try to resuscitate Murr when he stops breathing. They're talking as they try to save him, and I can't follow their words. Suddenly I flash back to the day I died. Until now, I had no memories of that day, or what happened to me.

Anna stands over my lifeless body as the EMTs try to bring me back. It's too late. I watch the whole thing as it unfolds, and it's strange how it's like watching a movie instead of myself. My best friend collapses as they cover my corpse with a white sheet and wheel me away on a gurney.

When the memory fades, I realize that they've just done the same with Murr. He's gone. I never got to tell him that I'd fallen in love with him. And he never finished researching a way for us to be together in a more permanent capacity. If I could cry, I would. But Jack has the ring, and he's busy talking to the EMTs right now.

I can't hear what they're saying, but I'm sure he's not telling them that his friend was murdered. They're probably going to play it off as an accident. Numbness settles over me; I haven't spoken since the emergency workers arrived. They wouldn't have heard me anyway, but everything felt too urgent and complicated for my words anyway.

Once the door closes behind them, and Murr's body has been removed, I stare out the window in shock. I can't believe this just happened.

I can hear Jack and Spence talking in the hall, but I don't understand what they're saying. An aching empty feeling surrounds me, and I can't resist closing my eyes and screaming at the universe for what it has taken from me. Arms wrap around me, and I'm pulled into a solid chest. But something is wrong. This isn't Spence or Jack.

My eyes fly open and meet a familiar brown pair of eyes. "Murr? But how?" I gasp. Jack and Spence rush into the room, stopping short when they see who's holding me.

"Kendall, are you okay? You were screaming, and I had to hold you. But I don't understand what's going on. I shouldn't be able to touch you without the ring." He turns his head and looks at the guys. "Thanks for saving me."

Tears stream down Jack's face, and Spence looks stricken. How does Murr not know he's dead? Wait; I know the answer to this one. I didn't know I was dead at first, either.

"Murr, honey, I'm so sorry," I say, hugging him tighter.

"For what? We're all here together now," he says with a smile.

MURRAY

"Murr, bud, we didn't save you. We tried; the EMTs tried. But your body didn't make it. You're dead," Spence tells me.

Jack wipes his eyes and nods. "It took too long to track you."

I shake my head. "No, guys, I feel fine. Really, I'm good." I turn back to the beautiful ghost in my arms. Oh, fuck.

Kendall looks up at me. "It was awful, but it's okay now. You're here with us, and we'll figure this out. I don't know how, but there has to be a way. Right?" She locks eyes with Spence, and he shakes his head slightly.

I don't miss the look on her face when his response registers. "Wait, you're serious? I'm dead?" I ask, reality setting in. I walk over to Jack and grab his arm, letting go as soon as I realize that he must have the ring.

I do the same with Spence, gasping when my hand goes right through him. "Oh, shit." Panic starts to grip me, and I can't think straight. I stumble away from them, falling through the wall into the back yard. Stopping for a moment to wonder what keeps me from falling through the ground, I walk over and sit under the tree, where I know Kendall goes to think.

It's not like anyone else can see me, so I won't cause any problems. I realize that while I'm panicking, my heart isn't pounding, and I'm not breathing heavy. Wow, I guess they're right. I'm dead. How shitty is it to die a virgin? I mean, damn.

What I don't understand is the reasoning behind it all. Who killed me? And why? After a few minutes under the tree, I realize that I'm calm again. No, I'm not calm. I'm pissed. More than that, I want answers.

Walking back to the house, I stop outside the back door, wondering if I should try to open it, or just walk through it. Fuck it—I'm dead. I might as well embrace it, right? I shrug and walk through the wall instead of the door. It's a strange sensation, but I keep going, searching the house for the others.

I find them in the living room, sitting on the couch. It's like they're waiting for me. "I'm sorry," I say when I float into the room.

"You have nothing to apologize for," Jack insists. "You've been through a traumatic experience, and it's a lot to process."

"I need answers," I blurt, cutting off whatever he was going to say next.

"Mama Nora attacked you here in the living room, then took you somewhere. I tried to warn you, then I tried to stop her, but I couldn't. I'm so sorry, Murr," Kendall says, her face contorted in pain. I hate that I'm the one who put that look on her face, but I can't take it away.

"The old witch?" I ask. "But why?"

"We're not sure, but she thought that getting rid of you would give her control of Kendall. I'm guessing she thought you had the ring. Since I had it when this happened, she didn't get what she was after," Spence explains.

"Fuck. That bitch killed me because she wants that ring?" I can't believe that I lost my life over a piece of jewelry.

"It's more than just a ring. It has half my powers inside it," Spence admits.

"What?" Kendall asks before I can. Jack doesn't look surprised by this announcement, so he must have already known.

"The witch was supposed to take my powers, but the ritual went wrong, and she only got half trapped in the ring. I think she wants the rest now, along with the ring. Which means she'll be trying to kill me now," he says. I don't know how they can be so fucking calm about all of this.

"What happens if she gets the ring and the rest of your powers?" I ask, actually feeling relieved that I'm dead so I'm not having a heart attack right now.

Spence shakes his head, and Jack answers, "We're not sure, but I would guarantee it won't be anything good. Spence discovered that his dad was a demon, too. The whole situation is fucked."

This is definitely a lot to process, and they keep adding to it. My best friend is a half-demon, and the ring that lets them interact with Kendall contains half of his power. What the actual fuck is going on here?

Kendall looks as confused as I feel, so I sit down next to her on the couch and thread my fingers through hers. "We'll figure it out, together." I hope my words are true, but right now, they're all I can offer.

She nods at me. "I know. And I'll help you figure out the whole ghost thing. It's not so bad when you have people to talk to." I consider the five years she spent isolated in this house, unable to leave.

CHAPTER TWELVE

ADJUSTMENTS

KENDALL

☐The next few days are a bit hectic. Murr's family comes for the visitation and funeral. I have no idea how he's keeping it together as well as he is. His family is tight knit, the exact opposite of mine.

"I just don't understand what happened," his mom says, crying on Jack's shoulder.

"I'm so sorry. I wish we could give you the answers you need," he responds, glancing at Spence.

Spence scowls and shakes his head. We all know that telling Murr's family the truth is a bad idea. It would put them all in danger. So, Jack and Spence do the best they can to comfort the family, while Murr and I watch.

"I can sense his spirit here, love," Murr's dad says to his wife.

I turn to Murr. "You have to stay calm. Let him think that you've come to say goodbye. Then we need to get as far out of the house as we can for a while."

I hate pulling him away from his family and the only closure he'll get. But I can't see giving them false hope or upsetting them with his rage.

"I'll try," he agrees. Pushing away the rage at being murdered by a witch isn't easy, and for a moment I think I'll have to drag him away without giving them a goodbye. Then, as if he knows what I'm thinking, he relaxes and smiles at his parents.

His eyes meet mine, and I nod. "I'm okay now. I can do this," he insists. I know that if he could cry, tears would be streaming down his face. I know if I could, I'd be sobbing.

As happy as I am to be able to touch him without the ring, I'm miserable knowing that he's dead because of me. I'll never be able to forgive myself for the pain I've caused his family, or him.

After he says goodbye to the people who raised him, who can't even hear his sweet words, he walks over and grabs my hand.

"Let's go," he says. I lead him into the back yard, as far from the house as possible. I hope it's far enough that his dad will sense him leaving.

JACKSON

Spence and I entertain Murr's family, comforting them the best we can. I watch as Kendall leads Murr out the back of the house.

His dad looks up and smiles. "He's moved on. His spirit is at rest."

As much as I want to tell him the truth, I can't. Instead, I let him think that his son's spirit has ascended. It will give them peace, the same way not knowing he was viciously murdered will.

Sometimes knowledge isn't power, it's pain. So, I vow to save them a much pain as I can, for as long as I can. Then I vow to take this witch out for what she's done. I'll do whatever it takes to make her suffer for all of this.

Once they're convinced that Murr has moved on, his family says a prayer and leaves. As soon as their cars pull away, Murr and Kendall come back inside.

"We need a game plan to hunt that bitch down," I say.

"It's not gonna be easy," Spence responds.

"I'm not looking for easy. I'm looking for justice," I growl.

Spence takes a step away from me, and Kendall steps between us. "We can't start fighting ourselves now. The only way to defeat her is to figure out what she's trying to do. Then we can find a way to stop it."

MURRAY

I stand back and listen as Kendall and the guys discuss how to go after the woman who killed me. I'm struggling with this whole situation.

"Why not just ask her what she wants? Make it sound like you're willing to deal. She doesn't have to know that you're not. At least not right away," I suggest.

They all turn to look at me. "I'm not sure if that's brilliant or completely stupid," Spence says with a smirk.

"Let's go with brilliant," I offer with a shrug.

"Could that really work?" Kendall asks.

"I don't know. But it's worth a try. She's made it clear to Spence that she's pretty desperate to make a deal with him. We may be able to use that to our advantage," Jack says.

I feel pretty good about my idea. Until I consider exactly what it means. "I changed my mind. It's a horrible idea. Don't do it," I say loudly.

"What the hell, man?" Spence asks. "That's the first good idea we've had since this started. Why do you want us to let it go?"

I shake my head. "She's dangerous. You'd have to go to her shop, alone, to offer the deal. She could kill you, too," I argue.

Jack paces the floor, considering my words. Spence laughs. "Nah. I'll be fine. I've been to see her by myself before. She can't hurt me. She needs me." I can't help thinking that his cocky attitude is going to get him killed. Just like me.

The difference is, I wasn't even cocky. I was just in the wrong place at the wrong time. "We all need to be on high alert. You can't assume that you'll be safe just because you were before. Look what happened to me. I should have been safe here," I answer.

"Murr is right. You guys have to be careful. I don't want anyone else to get hurt," Kendall says.

⁂

SPENCER

I have to admit, they have a point. But I still think that tricking Mama Nora into telling me what she wants my powers for is our best idea. Once we know, we'll be able to stop her for good.

I know that I'm being a little reckless, and I wonder if that's a demon attribute. I don't want to alienate these people who have become my family.

"If we can come up with another idea, I'll let this one go. But if not, this is what I'm going to do. I'll wait a couple of days. That's it. We can't afford to let her go unchecked for long. It's not safe," I say.

□I can't risk Mama Nora finding a way to steal my powers or recover the ring. We don't know what she wants either one for, but I'm not putting the entire city in danger because my friends are scared to face the witch. I'll do it myself if I have to.

□"No one is asking you to let it go. We just need to figure out a better way. I can't lose you guys," Kendall says. I want to pull her into my arms, but I can't, since Jack has the ring. I gesture to Murr, and he engulfs her in a hug. It's not the same, but it helps.

KENDALL

I let Murr distract me for a minute, and that gives Spence a chance to escape us. While I understand that he's worried about Mama Nora and whatever she has planned, we need to discuss options. Because I can't let Spence sacrifice himself.

"There has to be another way," I insist. Jack and Murr look at me. "We can't let him go up against her on his own. He can't defeat her by himself." I feel bad voicing my concerns, but I'm desperate for them to understand.

"Look, I'm all for finding another way, but I don't think there is one. Short of luring her here, so that you two are part of it too, I don't see another option," Jack says.

I'm losing this battle, and it terrifies me. I can't argue with anyone right now, so I force myself to fade away, reappearing in the attic space. I wonder for a moment if Murr will join me here since he's a ghost too, or if he'll stay in his room.

Another thought crosses my mind, and I laugh in spite of my sour mood. Now that Murr is a ghost like me, he has no reason to push me away anymore. Unless he just doesn't want me. I can't let myself consider that option. Sadness and worry are already trying to take over inside me.

I'm not sure how long I sit there, staring out the window, feeling lost. "Kendall?" Murr's voice pulls me from my trance. I turn to face him and realize that he's standing right behind me, almost close enough to touch.

"Are you okay?" I ask, understanding how difficult this transition is.

He shrugs. "Not really, but it's not like we can fix it. All I can hope for now is that the guys can find a way to bring you back so the three of you can be happy together."

His selfless declaration guts me. Because he's right. If they do manage to find a way to restore my life, I'll be giving Murr up. I don't want to lose any of them. "I don't want to think about a life without you," I say, wrapping my arms around his waist and burying my face in his neck.

He rubs his hands up and down my back. "It's okay, Kendall, if it happens, it'll be worth the sacrifice." We stand there, wrapped up in each other for a moment longer, then I lean back a little and look at him.

Murr smiles at me, but it doesn't reach his eyes. I lean up and press a kiss to his lips. He pulls me closer and deepens the kiss, fisting his hand in my hair. He's never been this forward with me, and I like it. My hesitant man takes control, guiding me back to the pile of pillows on the floor.

I don't fight him, submitting to his dominance. We've spent enough time together that I know he won't hurt me.

Once we're settled on the pillows, he finally breaks our kiss. It's impressive how long you can kiss someone when you no longer need to breathe.

"Kendall, I'm sorry I was so awkward before. I need to tell you something," he pauses, pressing a chaste kiss to my lips. I furrow my brow, waiting for him to continue. "I have no idea what I'm doing. I've only made out with a couple of girls before, and I've never had sex."

Wait, what? Murr is a virgin? "Is that why you always pushed me away?" I can't stop the question, or the hurt in my tone.

He gives me a guilty look, and I press my hand to his cheek. "I'm sorry. I didn't want to disappoint you, and it was really embarrassing to admit. Can you forgive me?"

I drag him back to me for another kiss, long and filled with passion. "There's nothing to be embarrassed about. If you want me, you can have me. If you're not ready, that's okay too. But don't ever be scared to tell me something."

Murr kisses me again, running his hands down my back and grabbing my ass. "Teach me what to do," he sighs against my mouth.

I hum against his lips while guiding his hands into new positions. If he wants to learn what I like, I'll definitely show him. "Are you sure?" I won't take advantage of him, though.

"I'm sure. I want you, Kendall," he says.

I spend the next hour or so getting both of us out of our clothes and showing him how I like to be touched. My fingers teach his how to stroke my clit, dipping inside of me and dragging my wetness out. He's a quick study, and before long, has me screaming in pleasure.

Guiding his hands along my skin gets me more worked up than usual, and as much as I want to take things slow, I know I can't. "I want to ride you," I say. His eyes widen and he grins.

□"Yes, please," he answers. "Show me what to do."

□I push him over on his back, climbing on top of him. He groans when I slide my slick core against his erection. I know that neither of us will last long, but this is what we both need. I sink onto him, taking him all the way inside me.

□I ride him slowly, lifting and lowering myself over and over until I can't hold my release back. As I fall over the edge, Murr flips me over and starts pounding into me. Apparently, I'm an excellent teacher. His thrusts prolong my orgasm, making it last until he catches up to me. "Kendall!" he cries out as he comes.

□When he's finished, Murr collapses on top of me, and I shudder. "That was incredible," I say against his shoulder.

CHAPTER THIRTEEN

COMPROMISE

KENDALL

Getting Spence to hold off on his plan to face Mama Nora on his own is difficult. Now that we know the ring holds half of his power, and that he's half demon, we need to approach things a little differently.

"I know we've been over this a dozen times at least, but what exactly did she say to you?" I ask, dragging Spence's attention back to me.

"That I'm the only one who can control the ring's power, because it's the other half of mine," he answers. His nostrils flare, and his eyes appear to flash red for a minute. I've never seen him do that before, and debate if I should mention it.

　Before I can decide, Jack speaks up. "Spence, have you noticed that your eyes flash red when you get mad now? I wonder if that's your demon powers surfacing since the witch told you about them."

　Murr and I exchange a look. Jack can't see us right now, because Spence has the ring. He's been trying to figure out how to control its power, but so far, isn't getting anywhere. He pulls it from his finger and hands it to Jack, then turns back to me.

　"Red eyes? Did you see it too?" he asks, his voice low.

　I nod, and he winces. "It's probably what Jack said. Or it's somehow connected to Murr's death. I've never seen your eyes do that before, so it has to be a new thing." Could Spence have gained power through that witch killing Murr?

　Before I can bring it up, Murr steps closer. "Spence, do you think that my death caused your power growth?"

　"Fan-fucking-tastic. Just what I need—more powers to figure out, and more to feel guilty about," he growls. I give Jack and Murr a look, causing them to step into the next room, giving me a minute with Spence.

　"I know this is a lot to process. But we can get through this together," I say once we're alone. He glares at me and I hold up my hands in surrender. "Or I can just leave you to it, I guess." I turn to walk away, but he clears his throat.

　"Wait," he says, stopping me in my tracks. "I'm sorry, Kendall. I'm so angry about everything. It's not an excuse for my behavior, but I'm struggling."

"I know. That's why I wanted to reassure you that I'm here for you," I insist, waiting a moment to turn back toward him. "But I can't help if you push me away. Neither can Jack or Murr."

"I feel responsible for everything, you know?" he admits.

"I know that feeling," I offer, glancing at Murr.

"But you didn't start all of this," he counters. "Just because we don't know yet how you're connected, that doesn't mean it's your fault. I'm the one Mama Nora wants; not you."

"You guys wouldn't have come across her if it wasn't for my death, and you moving in here. I can easily argue that I'm a catalyst in this, even if I'm not the main attraction," I argue with a smirk.

"Good point," he says. "I just don't want you to feel bad about what's happened."

"Same here, big guy," I respond.

JACKSON

We're all still adjusting to Murr being dead, and to his new ghostly form. I know it's been worse for him than for the rest of us. My biggest struggle is that I'm the odd man out now if Spence has the ring, because I can't see or hear Murr or Kendall. But it's not like I can ask Spence to let me keep the ring, since it technically holds half of his powers.

After Spence hands me the ring, Kendall gestures for us to give her a minute with him. They've been arguing a lot lately about who's responsible for all of this, and how we're gonna fix it.

Personally, I don't see a good solution here. I've begun to suspect that the ring is what killed Kendall, so I've been limiting my time with it. Which works out great, since Spence is trying to figure out how to control it. I know that I should tell the others about my thoughts, but I just can't bring myself to do it. I'm convinced that it will just be one more reason for Spence to feel responsible for everything.

The ring does have half of his powers, after all. And the only connection we've found so far between Kendall and the rest is that she found the ring at a pawn shop. Was that an accident, or something that was a well-considered part of Mama Nora's plan? I'm not sure we'll ever know.

Instead of focusing on that, I turn to Murr. "How are you adjusting?" I ask.

He gives me a sheepish grin. "It's weird, ya know? One day, I'm alive, sitting on the couch watching TV. The next, I'm dead, trapped in this house like our girlfriend."

I nod, and he continues. "I know this isn't gonna end well. Mama Nora is out for blood, obviously. I don't think there's anything else she can do to me or Kendall, but you and Spence are not safe. You guys have to protect each other," he insists.

"We will, Murr. And we'll figure out a way to bring you guys back," I say the words, even though we both know there is no way to do that. As much research as we've all done, we have not found any clues about how to bring back the dead.

□"Necromancy isn't the answer, Jack. You guys will have to let us go at some point. I hate being the one who says it, but there's not gonna be another way. We haven't found anything to indicate that Spence's powers can fix this. Death is permanent. It's not like being in a coma or just being sick for a while. At least it's not the end," he argues.

□I know he's right, but I hate it. It's killing me that we can't fix this. If only there was a way for Spence to absorb his powers again. Then we could take the witch out and that would be the end of all of this. Except that I would never see Murr again. Or Kendall. Fuck, I might not survive that.

SPENCER

□I don't want Kendall feeling responsible for our situation. I know all of this, everything that's happened since my father's death, is my fault. I may not understand how it all connects, but I can't get past the idea that Mama Nora is out to get me, and that she's killed more people than I know to make it happen.

□"I know you don't want me to do this, Kendall. And the last thing I want is to hurt you. But I have to at least talk to the witch about all of this. I need answers. We all do," I insist.

□"I don't know what I would do if anything happened to you," she admits. I can tell that she didn't' want to say the words. I completely understand the sentiment. I don't want to lose her either.

"What if I wear the ring when I go to see her?" I ask, thinking out loud. "Then I would have the full spectrum of my powers."

"That you don't remember or know how to use," she counters. It's a good point. I need more time with the ring before I hunt down the woman who keeps trying to ruin my life.

"So, I'll learn," I offer. Without giving her a chance to respond, I push past her, bumping my shoulder against hers as I walk out of the room.

"Spence?" she calls after me, panic lacing her voice.

"What?" I ask, turning back to face her.

"You just ran into me," she says.

"Oh, that. Sorry. I didn't mean to," I reply, the meaning of her words sinking in a few seconds later. "Wait, how? I can't touch you without the ring." With that realization comes a flooding of questions.

"Jack, will you come here?" Kendall calls. A moment later, Jack and Murr are standing in the room with us. "You have the ring, right?"

Jack nods. "Yeah, do you need it?" He offers me the ring, and I shake my head.

"I wanna try something without it," I answer, reaching a hand out toward Murr. I take a few steps forward, and my hand lands on his shoulder.

"How are you doing that?" Murr asks.

"I don't know. It has to be something with having the rest of my powers so close to me. Or because I've been using the ring so much." I turn to Jack. "You can still touch them, right?" I need to know if I'm draining the power from the ring, or if it's somehow duplicating.

Jack pulls Kendall into his arms, kissing her quickly. "I can," he grins. Leave it to Jack to use my question as an excuse to kiss our girl. Fuck, I can kiss our girl. Without the ring.

I drag Kendall out of Jack's arms, pressing her against my chest. Dipping my head, I capture her lips with mine. It should be awkward to be affectionate with her in front of the others, but it's not. I deepen the kiss, not wanting to let go of her. Something in me needs to memorize the feel of her, the taste of her, in case I never get to do this again.

Wait, am I anticipating this ending badly? What could possibly keep me away from Kendall? Murr is proof that even death wouldn't stop us from being together. I have to figure out what I'm really afraid of here, and then how to fix it.

When I pull back from the kiss, I smirk. "I would apologize, but I'm not sorry. This is an interesting development. We're gonna have to do a few experiments to see if the ring is getting weaker or if I'm just getting stronger. We really don't know enough about my powers—what they are exactly and how they work."

"So, you're not going after Mama Nora until we have time to do these experiments? I'd feel a lot more confident about sending you in there without back up if I knew that you could protect yourself," Kendall admits, looking up at me from where my arms are still wrapped tightly around her.

I kiss her forehead. "You have my word. I can't wait forever, but I'll give it some time to figure out what's going on here. We have to be ready in case she comes back, though."

"We can't let her hurt Jack the way she did Murr," Kendall agrees.

"I've been doing a little research on that, actually," Jack says, clearing his throat to remind us we're not alone. I reluctantly drop my arms from around Kendall.

"What did you find?" Murr asks, clearly not wanting to be left out of the conversation. "Is there something we can do to protect you?"

"There might be. I don't know a lot about witchcraft, but there are a few protection spells that might keep her from coming here. There are some that are specific to places or people. So, it depends on what we want to do. We can protect Spence and me, or we can protect the house. I'm not sure which is the better option right now," Jack explains.

"I like the idea of protecting both of you. What can she do with the house? Is there any real reason to worry about that?" Kendall asks.

CHAPTER FOURTEEN
GROWING POWERS

KENDALL

☐Jack thinks he's keeping secrets, but I've noticed how he doesn't want the ring as often as he used to. And I can tell from our time together, it's not me or Murr who have caused the shift. He's scared of the ring and its powers. I don't blame him. I might have felt that way, too, if I'd been aware of what I'd found at that pawn shop.

☐I can't regret my past choices, though. Everything I've done and everything that's happened to me has led me here, to these men who complete my soul. I can't remember being this happy ever, even if we are preparing to battle an evil witch who wants to steal one of my guys' powers.

　Every morning, I expect Spence to tell me it's time for him to seek out Mama Nora. It's been that way for weeks now. But instead, he settles in the basement or attic and practices with his new powers. I'm both terrified and relieved. The few times he's gotten angry, his demon side has made itself known more and more.

　"Spence, take a deep breath and calm yourself," Jack insists. He doesn't have the ring right now, so he can't see my amusement at him mothering Spence.

　Speaking of Spence, he's sprouted horns and his eyes are fully glowing red. Well, that's new. I can't say that I object to the aesthetic of it. Spence is a hot demon. The way those crimson horns circle around the side of his head, curving around his ears and stopping next to the base of his neck. I want to reach out and stroke them, to see if they're as sensitive as I suspect they would be.

　But as soon as Jack breaks through the anger, the horns recede. When Spence meets my gaze, he cocks and eyebrow, and I'm certain he knows exactly what I was thinking. Fuck. We don't have time for distractions.

　"I think I need a break, before I lose my temper completely," Spence says with a sigh. I've been encouraging him to pay attention to his limits, and I'm relieved to see that he's actually listening.

　"Good idea," I agree. I have a sudden urge to test something that's been working its way through my brain for a little while. "Will you try something for me?" He looks at me and shrugs. "Take Jack's hand," I say. "I want to see something."

Spence cocks his eyebrow again, but reaches out for Jack's hand. "Kendall wants to try something. I need your hand," he explains, since Jack can't see or hear me. I wonder if he realizes what I'm doing.

"Okay," Jack says, and it sounds more like a question than an agreement. But he puts his hand in Spence's anyway. It's nice to know that they trust me enough to do things without understanding what I'm thinking. "Now what?" He looks at Spence expectantly.

"Now I test my theory," I say, drawing Jack's attention to me.

"Kendall. I can see you and I heard you. How is this possible? I'm not even touching the ring," Jack says in awe. Just as I thought. Spence's powers are growing more every day.

"It's Spence. He's like a conduit for the power. Since it's his power, the connection with the ring is getting stronger the more he wears it. I figured with how he can touch me now when the ring isn't around, it might work the same if you touch him. I don't fully understand it," I admit.

"This is wild. So, if I let go," he says, letting go of Spence's hand. "Then I can't see you anymore. Okay." Jack grips Spence's hand again, then reaches for mine. "But can I touch you if he's holding onto me?"

I thread my fingers through Jack's, wondering exactly how this is working. Seeing spirits and talking to them is one thing but being able to touch him just because he and Spence are connected is weird. "This must be another power expansion."

Wanting to test another theory, I pull Jack away from Spence, my hand still firmly holding his. The moment their hands disconnect, I expect my hand to slide right through Jack's. When that isn't what happens, I gasp. "How?"

Spence grins at me. "I'm glad to know that worked. I was trying to push a little of my power into Jack while you were holding onto him. I have no idea how long it will work, or even if it would, honestly. But that's pretty cool, huh?"

JACKSON

Being able to touch, hear, and see Kendall without the ring is an amazing development. I can't help being concerned for any possible side effects of Spence sharing his demon powers with me, but I push that thought away. I'll worry about that later. For now, I'm going to enjoy holding our girl without outside magical assistance. Yes, I realize how dumb that sounds. I don't care.

I drag Kendall into my arms and hold her close. "I could get used to this," I admit.

"It is nice. But we have to keep in mind that it may not be permanent," Kendall reminds us.

"While we're playing around with Spence's powers, we should discuss how we're going to take down the witch," Murr suggests.

□Kendall shakes her head. "I'm not ready for that talk yet. Can we just focus on helping Spence learn his powers and get control of them? It's not realistic, but I really want to pretend for a little bit that we're just normal people. Well, as normal as we can be when two of us are ghosts and one is a demon-human hybrid."

□I can't help chuckling at her statement. It's ridiculous, but I understand her desire for the fantasy of a normal life. I would love to reassure her that we'll get there when all of this is over, but we all know that's not how this will end up. None of us is willing to voice that thought out loud, though. We don't want to admit that we'll have to say goodbye at some point.

MURRAY

□Spence's party trick is impressive. It makes me wonder what other powers he could pass along. Since he has maintained the ability to physically interact with myself and Kendall for a few days, I can't help considering that he's somehow absorbing the ring's powers. Especially if he can share those with Jack.

□"This is great, but can you do anything that will actually disable the witch from using her magic?" I ask, trying to circle back to the matter at hand. I know that Kendall doesn't want to discuss it, but we can't keep pretending that everything is okay.

⬛"I'm working on that," Spence says, forming a ball of fire in his hand as his fingers extend into red and black claws. It's impressive and terrifying at the same time.

⬛"Be careful with that. We don't need the house to burn down," Kendall insists. I stifle my laugh, because she's serious. I'm amused because she and I don't need the house. We don't eat or sleep, and rain or snow goes right through us. Cold and hot don't have much effect, either, so it's funny that she's worried about the house.

⬛I think about that for a minute. If the house was destroyed, would we still be bound here? It's an interesting thought, but then my brain goes worst case. We could be forced to move on instead of being able to go where we want. Okay, so destroying the house is probably not a good idea.

⚜

SPENCER

⬛I don't know how much longer I can put off going after Mama Nora. I know that she's been stalking us, but I don't tell the others. I've caught her watching the house a few times, and I make a mental note to get with Jack about those protection spells.

⬛The physical changes I'm going through are rough, and I consider calling Ma to see if she knows anything about them. I'm still upset that she kept things from me. Part of me understands why she did it, even if I disagree with her decision. If I had known I'm half demon, I might have been tempted to go after the witch on my own earlier.

As it stands, I'm not sure I can take her out on my own. But Jack doesn't have powers, and neither do Kendall or Murr. I wouldn't risk any of them anyway, so that's moot. Since I don't have anyone else to turn to, I have to find a way to do this on my own.

I understand Kendall's concerns about Jack and me staying safe and about protecting the house. I just can't let this go. And I can't spend much more time learning to harness my powers before I have to move. I don't tell my friends about my late-night practice sessions in the basement.

Since none of them have mentioned anything, I'm pretty sure my silence spells are working. If I can keep my plans hidden from them for just a little while longer, I may be able to execute everything before they have time to worry.

Kendall locks her eyes on me, and I'm nearly convinced that she can read my mind. I've been trying my best to be confident bordering on cocky to distract her from how dangerous this whole situation is. I don't need any of them trying to stop me from what I have to do. This is my fight, and I won't let it go. I need to take the witch out for what she's taken from me.

KENDALL

I have other theories about the ring and its powers, but I can't voice them just yet. If I do, it might push Spence to chase after the woman responsible for all of his pain. I'm not ready to risk having to say goodbye to him yet.

There's no way for the four of us to be together after the witch is defeated, other than the way things are right now. Well, there is one other way, but I'm not about to ask Spence or Jack to die for me. It's bad enough how excited I am about having Murr with me all the time. I'm constantly fighting a battle between joy and guilt. I love that I can see him, talk to him, touch him, any time I want. But I hate that he's dead because I couldn't stop that bitch from taking him.

I wish there was a way that I could go after Mama Nora myself. Unfortunately, being a ghost has more limitations than perks. Yeah, it's nice to not have to worry about doors or getting cold, but sometimes, it would be more useful to be able to move things or use weapons.

We've spent so much time on research and preparations already that I hate asking Spence to wait longer. I know he's been doing more practice than he's telling us about. Since I know he's safe when he's doing it, I haven't mentioned that I know. Let him think he has secrets.

I would love to talk to his mom about her secrets. For some reason, I'm convinced there's something else she's keeping from him. I'm not sure if it's about his father or herself, though. I can't have Spence ask her, because I think it would freak him out. The question and the answer.

I tuck those feelings away, hoping that what I'm thinking isn't written all over my face. I've wished a million times for things to be different, but we can't change the past. All we can do is work toward the future. And that means getting ready to go to war with a witch who has powers we don't know much about.

At least Spence is getting a handle on his demon side.

CHAPTER FIFTEEN

NO TIME LIKE THE PRESENT

KENDALL

WATCHING SPENCE PLAY AROUND with his powers is exciting. Under other circumstances, it would even be hot. But knowing that someone is out there, watching us, and waiting to make another move, creeps me out.

I don't think there's much she can do to me, or even to Murr now, but I'm terrified for Jack and Spence. More for Jack than anything, since he doesn't have any powers to protect himself with.

Spence has noticed the witch hanging around outside. I'm certain of it. Murr and I have been watching her. I'm teaching him how to be invisible, even to Spence. It may not be the most honest thing I've ever done, but we're learning a lot more about our situation than we would know if we didn't do it.

I trust Jack and Spence, and I know that they're just trying to do what they think is best. Hell, I'm not sure Jack even knows as much as Murr and I do. Spence is pretty secretive.

Movement across the street catches my attention. "Did you see that?" Murr asks, gripping my arm like a vice.

"I saw something. Not really sure what it was, though," I answer, scanning the street. Dark clouds roll in, as if a storm is coming. It seems unnatural somehow, making me uneasy.

Murr and I exchange a look before heading off to find Spence and Jack. "We should split up and get the guys to meet in the attic so we can see what's going on out there," I offer. Murr nods and vanishes through the floor, heading for the basement, where we last saw Spence. That means I have to get Jack. Let's hope that Spence's power is still working on him. Otherwise, I'm wasting time that we just don't have right now.

I find Jack in his bedroom, reading. It's completely out of character for him, but when I see the book title, I understand why. It's a spell book, and he's researching protection for the house and for them. "Jack, we need to meet the others in the attic," I say. "Mama Nora is outside, and things are getting weird." He doesn't flinch or acknowledge my presence. Fuck.

MURRAY

□Going to get Spence is easier than trying to convince Jack to come with me; especially since we don't know how long Jack will have the ability to see us before Spence needs to give him a boost.

□Plus, I've been wanting to practice melting through the floor for a while. When you're a ghost, there are very few ways to amuse yourself. I need to embrace enjoyment where I can.

□Once I'm in the basement, I glance around to find Spence in the corner with a book. He hasn't seen me yet, and I'm curious what he's reading. I take a moment to make myself transparent, the way Kendall taught me. Then I glide over to Spence and glance at the book he's holding.

□Interesting. It appears to be something about demons and how to defeat them. Is he preparing his defenses or looking for ways to die? That's a strange thought to have but would be a possible solution to our situation. If Spence died and was able to take his powers completely out of play, the witch would have nothing to go after.

□I shake my head, returning to my visible form. I can't let my friend contemplate suicide, can I? "Hey, Spence, we need you to come to the attic. The witch is outside, and some odd stuff is happening." As soon as the words leave my mouth, I realize that I should have announced myself. He jumps, dropping the book.

□I get a better look at the pages he was reading, and am fairly certain he was not, in fact, planning his death. "What's this?"

I ask, pretending that I hadn't already checked out his reading material.

"Murr, you gotta stop sneaking up on me like that," he says, putting a hand to his chest. "I've been studying possible powers and weaknesses so I know how to handle anything she throws at me." His voice is tinged with something akin to fear, and it makes me pause. I've never seen Spence rattled like this.

"Bring the book with you. We need to get upstairs. She's out there, and this might be happening sooner than we'd planned," I insist, gesturing toward the door.

JACKSON

I could have sworn that I heard Kendall for a minute, but when I look around the room, no one is there. Weird. Unless...has Spence's power transfer stopped working? I pause for a moment, considering what I think I heard. I have a sudden urge to go to the attic.

Well, what's the worst that can happen? I'm in the attic alone and look a little silly. I'll take that chance. Grabbing my notebook, pen, and the spell book I've been researching, I make my way upstairs, meeting Spence on the way.

"I guess I didn't imagine it, then?" I say, gesturing to the rush he seems to be in.

"Imagine what?" he asks.

 "That Kendall was trying to get me to go to the attic," I answer. "I think the power shift has worn off. But I had an overwhelming urge to go upstairs."

 Spence nods. "She's standing right behind you. And Murr is, too. The witch is outside, apparently, and she seems to be preparing to attack. We need to get ready."

 Once we're in the attic, I set up the supplies we'll need to cast the protection spells. As I'm working, Spence walks over and puts his hand on my shoulder. This time, I feel a pulse of electricity shoot through me. when I look up, I can see Kendall and Murr. They look more solid than they did the last time Spence shared his gift with me. I don't have time to wonder what this means. We have work to do.

 A thought hits me, and I stop what I'm doing. "Hey, Spence. You can touch Kendall and Murr, right?" He looks at me, processing my question for a moment.

 "Fuck, why didn't I think of that?" he mutters, stomping over to our ghost companions. A moment later, they seem even more solid than before, if that's possible. It amazes me when Spence understands what I'm thinking without me voicing it.

SPENCER

 With Jack settled, I have to focus on figuring out exactly what Mama Nora is doing outside. I kick myself for a moment as I walk to the window. I should have realized that I could transfer power to Kendall and Murr the same way I do to Jack. Now the four of us can fight together in physical form.

What I see out the window stops me in my tracks. This is bad. It's worse than we expected. The witch is conjuring a storm outside of our house. That's not the concerning part. I'm worried when I realize what the storm is made up of.

"Guys, we have a problem," I say, drawing their attention to the scene outside.

Three bodies crowd against me, following my gaze and gasping when they see what I'm seeing. Creatures and beasts swirl in the dark clouds. When the black drops of rain start to fall, each one turns into a spectral spider. Waves of them attack the house, shaking its foundation.

"We're not safe here," Kendall insists.

I think for a moment that she's forgotten about being a ghost. She and Murr are stuck here; they can't leave the property. And I won't abandon them, so we're gonna have this battle here.

As much as we've practiced and prepared, I don't feel ready. It's not like I can run off and wait for another day. This is happening now, ready or not. I can't let my family down. I have to protect them. And that means embracing the things I've been doing in the basement on my own, no matter how much they scare me.

"I'm gonna do something, and it's probably gonna look pretty scary. I need you all to trust me," I say, glancing at each of them. Kendall and Murr nod at me.

"We trust you," Jack insists. Their unwavering support bolsters me against what I need to do.

"I'm gonna need a little space for this," I warn, and they all step back, heading toward a window on the other side of the room.

Taking a deep breath, I let my demon powers take over. Horns sprout from just above my temples, curling around my ears. My skin turns red, and I can feel the flames licking my skin. It doesn't burn, but it's hot.

Throwing my head back, I release a feral scream. When I look out the window again, my eyes meet Mama Nora's and I see the first hint of fear in her dark orbs. Good. She needs to be scared, since I plan to eat her soul before this ends.

Wait, what was that? I want to eat her soul? That's some disturbing shit, even for me. I push that thought away, trying to get a handle on my demon powers. Inside the house is too cramped for my demon form. I need to get outside.

Glancing around the room, I see the widened eyes of my companions. "I won't hurt you, not intentionally," I rasp out, hearing the new echo and gravelly tone that comes from inside me.

"Spence, is that still you?" Kendall asks, taking a step toward me before Murr's hand on her arm stops her.

I smile but fear it's more of a grimace with their reaction to it. "I'm still in here. But I need to stretch." I gesture at my hunched shoulders that are nearly touching the ceiling.

"How are we gonna get you out of here without destroying the house?" Jack asks. In response, I concentrate for a moment, shrinking myself nearly to the size of a common house cat. "Oh, that is a neat trick!" he exclaims, opening the window enough for me to climb out, then slamming it shut before I can order him to.

I'm relieved that they understand how big a threat these shadow spiders could be. The house is still shaking from time to time as they climb the outside, looking for a way in. Now that I'm out in the open, I stretch myself to my full size, climbing easily to the roof. This vantage point is perfect for thwarting the witch's attacks.

I send my demon fire out, coursing along the roof and down the outside of the house. It burns away the shadow spiders without harming the house. I'm thrilled at how well Jack's protection spells are working right now. My powers don't seem to be able to damage the building at all.

KENDALL

Seeing Spence's demon transformation is unnerving to say the least. We've seen hints of his additional form during training sessions when he's nearly lost control of his temper. I was not expecting him to grow almost four feet taller and a foot wider, turn red, and sprout horns. And I'm pretty sure he might have wings now, too, but with the attic being so cramped, I couldn't tell.

"That was...a lot," I manage to say after Jack lets Spence out the window.

□"His demon form is magnificent," Murr responds, staring out the window in awe. I'm not sure if he's amazed or turned on right now. And since Spence gave us a bit of his power, Murr's cheeks are the prettiest shade of pink as he gushes over the demon who is on top of our house, protecting us.

□I have to admit, the sight of Spence transforming got me going too. It doesn't surprise me that Murr is into it as well.

□We all move closer to the window to watch as Spence faces off against Mama Nora. The whole attack is strange. I'm not sure how no one can see what's going on. □

CHAPTER SIXTEEN

COLLATERAL DAMAGE

SPENCER

When I shifted, I expected this form to be hard to hold onto. I anticipated the effort exhausting me, and I'm pleasantly surprised when the opposite happens. The longer I stay in this form, the stronger and more powerful I feel.

Mama Nora keeps sending shadow creatures to attack the protection spell we put on the house. I knock them out easily, starting to get bored with all of this. I need to take her out already and put an end to the fight.

Before I can figure out how to sneak up on her, I'm tackled off the roof by something large and furry. I hit the ground hard, with this beast on top of me, its teeth inches from my neck. Shit, how did this thing surprise me?

Mentally kicking myself for getting distracted, I wrestle with the large beast, trying to figure out what it is. It reminds me of a dog or a wolf, but supersized. Just as the shadow beast's teeth sink into my arm, I realize why it looks so familiar. Its red eyes bore into me, and I recall the book I'd been studying just yesterday.

This monster, this hell hound, is one of very few that produces a venom that's poisonous to demons like me. I'm completely fucked here. Once the beast's teeth puncture my skin, it disappears, leaving me dizzy and weak. Just as my vision starts to go dark, I hear the witch laugh, calling out to the hound—did she just call the thing 'Pookie'? —as a strange sound fills my ears and debris falls around me.

KENDALL

We watch in horror as Spence falls from the roof with some kind of dog monster on top of him. "We have to help him," I insist, zipping down to the main floor for a better view point. Murr is at my side in an instant. It seems as if Spence's power he shared with both of us has faded, since we're able to move through the walls and floor again.

I hear Jack coming down the stairs as the house starts to glow. "What the fuck?" Murr says as the glow gets brighter, nearly blinding now. At the moment I squeeze my eyes shut at the glare, I hear cracking. Suddenly, a deafening boom hits. My eyes fly open as glass shatters around us. Wood splinters and shoots outward as the top of the house collapses in on itself after the lower walls disintegrate.

◻I blink a few times to clear my vision. My head whips around to where Spence is laying in the yard, unmoving. Fuck. I scan the street, searching for the witch, but she's gone. Desperation grips me as I race to Spence's side.

◻I try to touch him, but my hand falls right through his chest. "Spence, please, don't leave me." I'm not ashamed to beg him to stay. I look up from his body to see the house in shambles. Murr and Jack walk out of the rubble, unscathed somehow, except for the shocked look on their faces. I can't imagine that seeing Spence like this is easy for either of them, though.

◻"I can't move him. Jack, come help," I call to them when they stop at the bottom of the porch steps. Jack and Murr stare at me as if I've missed something important. "Come on, Spence is hurt. We need to get him somewhere safe."

◻Murr's eyes go wide and I feel like he's trying to tell me something. "Spence is okay, Kendall. But we need to talk to you," he insists, glancing at Jack.

◻"We can talk after Jack moves Spence somewhere safe," I insist.

◻Jack steps forward and my jaw drops as Murr grabs his arm to stop him. Spence's power must still be working for Jack. Then why did it stop for Murr and me? None of this makes sense. "I have to tell her," Jack insists, shaking Murr off.

"Tell me what?" I ask, finally turning my attention away from Spence long enough to lock eyes with Jack.

"I'm dead, Kendall. I won't be able to touch him either," Jack says.

"What?" I ask, refusing to believe what Jack is telling me, even as he walks over and pulls me into his arms. "No, no, it's not possible. Stop joking around."

Instead of answering me, he kneels next to Spence and puts his hands through our unconscious companion's chest. Shit, this is bad. "I wish it was a joke," he says, looking at me again.

His eyes are filled with pain and sorrow. Guilt tears through me again, just like it did with Murr. This is my fault. If I had avoided that ring when I found it in the pawn shop, maybe none of this would be happening. What the fuck do we do now?

A groan sounds next to us as Spence stirs. "That fucking hurt," he mutters. "I feel sick." Before he's fully aware of what's going on, Spence rolls onto his side and vomits on the grass. He flops back again, covering his eyes with his arm as his demon form shrinks down and fades away.

I have no idea how long we wait for him to open his eyes again. My eyes stay locked on the shallow rise and fall of his chest. I have no idea what will happen to his powers if he dies, but I don't think it will be good.

Rain starts to fall, and Spence finally sits up. The movement seems to take a lot of effort for him, and I hate that we can't help. He glances around where the three of us surround him, then past us to the house. "Fuck," he says as he stares at what's left of our home. His head whips over to look at Jack. "No, Jack, I'm so sorry. This is my fault."

JACKSON

I flinch at Spence's apology. "You aren't the one who killed me. You didn't even start this fight. It's not your fault that we ended up being collateral damage in a war you never asked for," I argue.

Being dead is weird. Dying hurt, I won't lie about that. There's no way a building falling on you isn't going to be painful. But that's over now, and Spence is not responsible for what happened.

"No, but it may be my family's fault," he replies. "I'm pretty sure my mom is hiding things from me still. I suspect there's more to my father's death than we know."

I'm not sure what makes him think that, but he hasn't exactly been sharing things with us lately. "The important thing now is to keep the witch from getting your power. I won't lie and say I'm happy to be dead, but there's nothing you can do about it."

I'm surprising myself with my attitude on this. I refuse to let Spence blame himself and spiral into a position that will let the witch win. We don't know what she wants his power for, though.

"Maybe you should talk to her," I suggest after talking a minute to consider the situation. Spence's mom might know what the bitch wants. Even better, she may know a way to stop her. Hopefully one that doesn't involve Spence dying too.

"That's actually a great idea. It's too bad we can't go with you," Kendall says, pacing wide circles as she listens to us talk, each pass getting bigger and bigger.

"Maybe we can," Murr says, pointing to where Kendall stands in the street.

Her eyes go wide when she realizes that she's no longer on the property. I wonder if the house being destroyed has broken the binding that held my friends here. The one that no doubt would hold me here too, if it still exists.

Murr takes a few steps toward Kendall, slow and hesitant. When he reaches the property line, there's a faint glow at his feet but he walks right over it with no reaction.

Without pausing, I dart over to Kendall, wincing as I cross the glowing line, half expecting some unseen force to drag me back and away from our girl. When it doesn't happen, I laugh.

"We can go with him," I say.

KENDALL

Jack's realization that we're no longer tethered to the house or property is amazing. I hadn't realized how far away from the house I'd walked while I was pacing around. I just couldn't stand still while they discussed everything. I felt a buzzing inside of me, and I needed to move. Once I got into the street, it eased up.

□"I wonder if that disconnection is what I felt that made me have to move," I say out loud.

□Murr looks at me and grins. "I felt the weirdness too, but didn't realize what it may have been. I just thought we were getting overwhelmed by everything."

□"We need to get moving, then. I want to talk to my mom, and you guys may be able to help me drag answers out of her that she might not want to give," Spence says.

□On the way to Spence's mom's place, the guys discuss strategy for getting Mrs. Richardson to spill her guts. I'm too distracted to pay attention to their conversation. This is the first time in five years that I've been able to leave home, and I'm staring out the car window, fascinated by everything. Honestly, it's a little ridiculous how excited I am about just being able to leave the property.

□I don't care, though. I watch as we pass the park, where kids are playing, and dogs are running. If any of them could see me, I'm sure they'd think I'm insane with the way I'm grinning at everything. The guys don't seem to notice me at all, and I'm okay with that. I think they understand that I need a little time to adjust to this newfound freedom.

SPENCER

After parking on the street, I walk into my mom's apartment building and enter her apartment without knocking. Normally, I wouldn't be so forward, even with my mother, but I can't risk her refusing to let me in. I want answers, and she's going to give them to me.

Once we're inside, I corner Ma in the kitchen. I have the other start nosing around in other rooms. I'm not sure if Ma can see ghosts or not, so I'm trying to keep her away from them if possible.

"Spencer! What a lovely surprise! Would you like some tea?" The look on her face is genuine happiness at seeing me. Part of me hopes that she doesn't lose that look when I tell her why I'm here.

"Ma, we need to talk about some stuff. Tea would be great, but I'm here for answers," I begin. Her eyes meet mine and she nods. I wonder if she knows what I'm going to ask already.

"I knew you wouldn't leave it alone, son. I'll make tea, and we'll talk," she answers, turning back to the stove and grabbing her kettle. I give her time to process while she makes the tea, answering her small talk and pretending that things are normal.

When she sets the tea tray on the table and takes a seat, she heaves a sigh before meeting my gaze. "You already know that your father was a demon, and that he helped create the ring." At that point, she notices that the ring in question is on my finger. "I see you got it back. Good. They're your powers, and you should have them."

◻She clears her throat, busying herself with pouring tea for us. "We tried to take your powers that day, but this whole thing started years before that. Right after I graduated college, I was desperate to start a family. I felt as if I had no options, so I turned to Mama Nora for help. She convinced me to summon a demon and make a pact. Then she helped me trap your father. I don't think she expected us to fall in love, but we did. Part of the pact involved giving her my firstborn child. I couldn't let her have you, so we made a new bargain."

CHAPTER SEVENTEEN
SAY WHAT NOW?

KENDALL

AFTER GOING THROUGH THE apartment with Jack and Murr, we realize that there's no point in us snooping. We can't physically interact with anything, so unless she's left something out in the open, we won't find it.

Since we don't know yet if Spence's mom can sense us, we have to stay out of the room they're in. So, we're eavesdropping. It's juvenile and pointless, but at least Spence won't have to fill us in on everything his mom is telling him.

◻"You decided at twenty-one that you had no options for having a family besides summoning a demon?" he asks, anger lacing his tone.

◻"I don't expect you to understand, but yes. I'd been through some trauma when I was younger and didn't think I could have children. When I discussed the issue with Mama Nora, she suggested an alternative. I knew the cost when I made the deal. But after I had you, we couldn't give you up. I never expected to fall in love with your father. He was supposed to just be a means to an end," she answers.

◻This is some fucked up shit, but honestly, it doesn't surprise me. Spence talked about how in love his parents were. I'm sure it's a shock to find out that your father isn't who or what you thought. I can't imagine being part demon is easy.

◻"Okay, fine. But what about the others? How are they connected? It's not a coincidence that the three of us guys ended up living where Kendall died. I can't help feeling like it goes back further than that, too. So, you're gonna tell me how each of them relates to all of this," Spence insists.

◻His mom sighs heavily, and I think for a minute that she's going to avoid the question. "Why don't you ask them to come in here and we'll have this conversation together?"

◻Jack, Murr, and I exchange a look, my eyes going wide. "Did you hear that?" Spence calls to us. We slide through the wall, moving to surround Spence where he sits at the table. "I guess that means you can see them, too?" he asks her.

◻"It's not exactly the same as your power, but yes, I can see that they're here. I don't know if I can hear them, but I'm certain they can hear me. And that will be enough for this," she explains.

"I'm sorry, Spence. We tried not to get too close," I say, staring at his mom to see if she reacts.

"Did you hear that?" he asks her, ignoring my apology.

"It's like a static noise. I know it's there but can't make it out. Like their shapes—I can't see them well enough to know who is who, but I can see a blob that shouldn't be there." Her explanation makes sense, and I'm kinda relieved that she can't hear me.

"Okay, now that we know what we're dealing with, you can tell your story. I'll relay anything relevant that they say or ask," he offers, encouraging her to start talking.

"For starters, Kendall's mother made a deal with your father before I did. I don't know the details, just that the deal involved suffering a loss at an inconvenient time. I'm not sure if she has now or had any supernatural abilities when she was alive," she pauses as if she's trying to figure out which blob is me.

"As for the boys, that one is a bit more complicated. Since Jack never manifested his powers, and Murr's didn't end up the way they were supposed to," she finishes with a wave of her hands.

"What do you mean? We were all supposed to have powers? How?" Spence tosses the questions at his mother while Murr and Jack stare at her in confusion.

"I mean, it's complicated, but technically they are your brothers. Your father is, was, their father, too, in a way. Please don't ask me about all of that. It was a horrible mess, and we'd rather not relive it all. Just know that we love you boys more than you'll ever realize. And yes, they have human "dads" but that doesn't mean anything biologically speaking," she says.

"Wait, is she saying that all three of you are half-demon?" I ask, locking eyes with Spence.

"Ma," he starts, getting her to look at him. "You're gonna have to explain that. Because it sounds like you're saying the three of us are half demon, and I feel like we might have noticed that a little earlier."

She shakes her head. "Like I said, it's complicated. But no, not all of you are half. Best I can tell, Murr is a quarter, and Jack is somehow less than that on the demon side of things. It's not like magic follows the rules of genetics or anything. And to be fair, I'm pretty sure you are more than half-demon, son," she insists.

"I really don't want to go into this, especially without the other mothers here. But I will tell you this—the three of us did what we thought was best for you boys, and we would do it again. All we ever wanted was healthy children. It's what led us to the choices we made. And maybe I don't know all the details. It's possible that Jack's mom bargained away his powers. You'd have to talk to her about that," Spence's mom says quietly.

I can tell that she doesn't want to talk to us anymore, and I understand her hesitation. This is a lot to discuss, and it's even more to process. Each of our families made a deal with a demon for something they wanted. It seems like my family was the only one who did it for selfish reasons. That is disappointing but not surprising.

SPENCER

☐"Ma, none of this makes sense. You were so young. Why would you think a demon was the only way for you to have kids?" I can't help asking, even though she's said repeatedly that she doesn't want to discuss it. And what little she's explained hasn't answered the question.

☐"Spence, I don't want to unload my trauma on you. But I understand that you need answers. The truth of it is, I was raped when I was nineteen. It was a violent assault, and I came out of it close to death and pregnant at the same time. I wasn't emotionally equipped to deal with having my assailant's baby, so I had an abortion. A year later, I found out that the doctor who did the procedure had damaged my uterus, and that there was little chance I'd actually be able to have a baby. There was nothing the doctors or medical advances could do to fix that, son. I was desperate, and did what I thought I had to," she admits. Learning this about my mother is painful, but I know there's no way around it. We need answers so we can prepare to deal with Mama Nora.

☐"I didn't realize when I made the deal that I was agreeing to give you to her. The wording of it all made me think I was giving up my most valued possession. I thought that meant your grandmother's ring, not my child." Her words floor me.

"I never would have made the deal if I had known it would turn out this way. Your father gave his life so the witch wouldn't take you from me. The only reason she agreed was because she was supposed to get all of your power in addition to his lifeforce. I'm so sorry," she cries, covering her face with her hands.

"Wait, so all this time, I thought you tried to take my powers to make my life better, and that wasn't what happened at all?" I ask, my jaw gaping.

She shakes her head. "I'm sorry. We had to tell you something, and your powers were not the most convenient thing to deal with in public school. It wasn't like we could explain to the teacher that you weren't talking to your imaginary friends, but ghosts of people who'd been killed and sought you out for help."

I guess I can understand that part of it. But I hate that she lied to me. I take a deep breath, locking eyes with Kendall. She smiles at me, and I know without a doubt, that I'll forgive my mother for what she's done. None of it matters, anyway. We still have to get rid of the witch.

"I know you don't want to tell us someone else's story, but Ma, we need to know how and why the others have been dragged into this. You said Kendall's mother made a deal for power. Did that include giving up Kendall's life?" As much as I don't want her to hear the answer, Kendall needs to know. From the look on her face, she's already convinced of the worst.

Ma nods. "It did. It was even her mother's idea. 'I'll trade my daughter's life for more power,' she offered. Of course, your father couldn't say no to that. He survived on the souls of people he made deals with. It wasn't something he took lightly, though. He assured me that it would be done in the most painless way possible. It seems that his death may have changed that a bit."

This is all too much to process. I don't know how Kendall and the guys aren't freaking out right now. "What about Murr and Jack? Did their moms have similar stories to yours?" The question is out before I can stop it.

Tears stream down Ma's cheeks now. "I don't know the details, but Murr's parents had tried for so long to have a baby with no luck. Mama Nora's deal gave them a chance at that. When Jack's mom was pregnant with him, she discovered that he was ill. The doctors wanted her to terminate the pregnancy. She couldn't bear the thought of giving up her sweet baby, so she made a deal as well. That could be why he doesn't have powers at all."

JACKSON

Everything is moving so quickly; I've barely had time to process the fact that I'm dead. My body is crushed under what's left of our house. I stand there, listening to Spence and his mom discuss everything until I just can't take it anymore. And without anything binding me here, I walk away. I'm not leaving them forever; I just need some space for a few minutes.

☐Kendall has had more than five years to adjust to life after death, I've had a couple of hours. Even Murr seems to be taking things better than I am. I won't tell them how I feel, but I'm freaking out about all of this. My mom made a deal with a witch and a demon because I wasn't going to be born healthy, or possibly at all.

☐I don't know how to feel about any of it. It's one thing to be able to confront your parents about what they did. It's completely another to realize that you'll never get to talk to your parents again. Sure, I can be there when they find out that I'm gone, but I can't pull Mom into my arms and hug her or even tell her that it's okay. For one thing, it's not okay. For another, I'm fucking dead.

CHAPTER EIGHTEEN

ONE LAST FIGHT

KENDALL

☐Armed with the knowledge of what our parents did, we leave Spence's mom to regroup and figure out how to kill Mama Nora once and for all. Even though we didn't learn anything new about my mother's involvement, at least we know how the guys are connected. I'm not even sure I care anymore about my family and their shady dealings.

On the way back to what's left of our house, I notice that Jack is more quiet than he has been in a while. I know that he's struggling with what just happened to him, and what we learned, but I don't know how to help him with it. My heart aches for what he's going through.

"Well, you're the only one who can kill the witch," Murr says, staring at Spence. "It's not like the rest of us can physically interact with her at all. Unless you share your powers with us, I guess."

"That's too physically taxing on him," I argue, not wanting Spence to drain himself before we go up against our foe.

We get out of the car and approach the ruins that were our home. It seems strange to me that no one bothered to call the cops or make sure no one was hurt.

"Let's not argue about it. Ma gave me something that was my father's, and I think I know what I have to do," Spence says, heading toward the destroyed building where we used to live. Instead of going inside, he heads around the house to the back yard. When he stops at my favorite tree, I wonder what he's doing.

"I'm not sure about this, Spence," Jack says. "Maybe you should just run away. It'll be safer than facing off against the witch."

Spence looks up at Jack from where he's kneeling beside the tree. "I'm not running. It's gonna be okay, Jack. Trust me. She won't get my power. We're not gonna let that happen."

I move closer and see that Spence has pulled a small book out of his pocket. "Is that what your mom gave you?" I ask.

He nods. "Part of it, anyway. I need to read this to figure out exactly how to use the weapon Ma gave me. All I know is that it has the power to end this. I need you guys to keep an eye out while I read, so Mama Nora doesn't sneak up on me. Can you do that for me?"

We agree and take a few steps away to give him some privacy. I'm desperate to know what kind of weapon his mom gave him, and why it would be confusing for him to figure out how to use it. But I'll give him time and space to read the book and discover what he needs to know before I start asking too many questions.

Jack and Murr stand on the other side of the tree, watching the front of the property, while I keep an eye on the back.

⁂

MURRAY

"I don't have a good feeling about this," I say to Jack. "I think he's hiding something from us."

"Agreed, but without knowing what he's reading, it's hard to tell," he responds.

"Did it seem to you like he was saying goodbye to his mom in a more permanent capacity when we left?" I can't stop myself from asking what's been weighing on me since we walked out of Spence's mom's place.

Jack looks at me and his eyes go wide. "He can't. Maybe he's just preparing for the worst? There's no way he can be going into this expecting to die. Just because the witch took you and me out, and indirectly, Kendall, too, that doesn't mean she can kill him."

"He's strong, for sure. And his powers are growing, but I feel like he's keeping things from us and I don't like it. I wish we'd had more time to discover our powers," I admit.

"They said I didn't have any because I was sick. Why wouldn't Mom tell me about being sick? It's not like she would have needed to tell me about her deal. She could have just said that the doctors made me better or it was a miracle. I can't even ask her about it now," he says.

I feel bad for him, because even though I didn't get to tell my parents goodbye, at least they got a little closure when they had my funeral. From the way things look here, Jack may not get one—at least until after all of this is over. And who knows where we'll be at that point?

❦

JACKSON

I suspect that Spence is planning to sacrifice himself somehow during this last face off with Mama Nora. I understand that he probably thinks that's the best option. I'm not sure that would keep the witch from getting his powers, though, and I don't want to see that happen. Even if it would solve our issues, it wouldn't stop the evil woman from hurting innocent people. Who knows what she has planned for Spence's powers? I don't want to be responsible for her getting them.

Movement in front of the rubble that was our house catches my attention. "What's that?" I gesture to the flashing lights a moment before we hear sirens.

"Someone finally called emergency services about the house. Fuck, how are we supposed to protect Spence when the cops are probably gonna try to question him about this? Especially when they find your body," Murr says, rushing to Spence to let him know what's going on.

I head to the front of the house to check out what's happening out there. A crowd gathers, and there are firemen digging through the remains of the house. At this rate, they might find my body before Spence figures out how to defeat the witch.

Of course, the moment I have the thought, it's dashed by the lightning that strikes inches from the house.

<hr>

SPENCER

I know Mama Nora is here before Murr and Kendall tell me about the magical lightning that's striking around the house, where firemen are trying to sift through the rubble for survivors. I want to tell them it's pointless, but then I'd have to explain about my powers, and I'm not having that conversation.

Instead, I try to finish reading as much of my father's journal as I can. I need to destroy the ring and reabsorb my power before Mama Nora gets to me. There won't be a way to hide the magic from the bystanders, so I'll have to move quickly. I need to do my best to protect them, even if it's impossible.

□*The most important part of the ritual is your intent. If you do not have a specific intent in mind, the ritual will not work. For transfer of power, you must want to transfer the power from one vessel to another. If that desire is not present, the transfer will not work. If two people are performing the ritual together, and have different intents, the results could be disastrous.*

□Well, that's good to know. My intent is to keep the witch from getting my powers, no matter the personal cost. That's easy enough to settle on. What next?

□*Once your intent is set, you must focus on the power contained in the first vessel and pull (into yourself) or push it toward the intended target. Don't be alarmed if the first vessel is destroyed when the power is removed from it. This does include any magical being. Use this ritual with caution if you care at all about the vessel you are removing power from.*

□His words stop me in my tracks. This has to be the ritual they performed to take my powers. There's no way it isn't. Does that mean that his intent was different from that of Mama Nora? Is that why I kept part of my powers? I have so many questions and no one to ask.

□*The only way to destroy power is to destroy the vessel completely. If a vessel is destroyed by another magical being, that being may be able to absorb its power. If the intent is to prevent a transfer of power, then the vessel must be destroyed with a meteorite dagger. That is the only substance that can destroy a magical being and their power.*

Great, so I can either try to kill the witch with the dagger my father left me, or I can use it on myself. Either way, someone dies. Logically, I know that death is inevitable, but that doesn't mean I'm ready for it. Or am I?

If I did this, it would make a lot of things easier. I would ensure that the witch didn't get my powers. I'd be able to touch Kendall whenever I wanted. The four of us would finally be together without someone being left out. My thoughts are mostly selfish, but I can't help how I feel. Can I really be considering this? It's one thing to think about it, it's another to actually kill yourself; especially with a dagger. This would be easier if one of the others could stab me.

I know that's not gonna happen. I can't even let them know about this plan. They'll do everything they can to stop me or talk me out of it. I know this is the best option, though. It involves the least amount of collateral damage. A strange feeling of calm settles over me after my decision is made. I pocket the book, making sure the dagger is within easy reach. Then I head toward the front of the property, where the emergency workers are digging Jack's body out.

I don't know how I'll avoid questions about what happened, but I have to try. I walk past the emergency personnel who are digging out my best friend's body, my resolve strengthening with every step. Jack didn't deserve what was done to him here. And I'm going to make it right. I can't fix it by bringing him back to life, but I can make the witch pay. So, that's what I'm going to do.

I stop at the corner of the demolished structure, remembering that I need to destroy the ring and absorb its power before I continue with my plan. I peek around the side of the rubble, watching firemen struggle to search for survivors and remains. My eyes scan the area for Mama Nora. When I don't see her, I relax a little. Kendall, Murr, and Jack are keeping watch for me. They'll let me know if they see her, and I'll be ready when they do.

I grip the ring in my hand, focusing on turning myself into shadows. I can't use my demon powers in the open without risking the lives of innocent people, but if I'm obscured from their view, it has to be enough. Once I'm certain the humans on the property can no longer see me, I turn my attention to the ring resting on my shadowy palm.

I need to make sure my intent is locked in my mind. I will destroy this ring and absorb its power. Taking a few calming breaths, I feel my heart racing as I start to squeeze the thin metal band. I'm not sure if I have enough strength to break the metal or not, but I have to try.

Voices carry to me as I crush the ring in my palm. "She's here, Spence, hurry," Kendall insists. She sounds terrified, and I wonder if that's because of me or the witch. No matter; I have to focus on taking my power back from its prison before I face off with this witch.

"We're out of time," Jack yells. I flinch as dark red tendrils start to dig into my flesh as they fight free of the mangled metal band on my palm. Reclaiming my powers is painful. I'll take it, and more pain before this day is finished. I can't let the witch win. Focusing my attention back to my powers, I pull them into me, dropping the drained metal onto the ground as I lift my head and step toward where Kendall and Jack's voices came from.

⁂

KENDALL

□Spence's eyes glow red when he drops the shadows from around himself. I'm certain that he's absorbed the ring's power back, and while the thought scares me, I know he's gonna need it. I'm not naïve enough to believe that he's not planning to take himself out if it comes to that. I just hope it doesn't get to that point. I want him to destroy the witch so she can't hurt anyone else.

□If only I knew how to make that happen. The chaos around us of emergency personnel working and police investigating falls away as our attention zeroes in on Mama Nora and the swirl of lightning that surrounds her. Seriously, how is no one else seeing this?

□I get distracted trying to figure out how the humans are just going about their day as if there's not a magical face-off happening twenty feet away. Spence yells something at Mama Nora, and they both step closer. This is really happening, and I have no way to stop it.

□"Give me the power, and no one else will get hurt," she insists.

□"You lie. We both know that the only reason you want my power is to hurt people," Spence argues.

□I know that he's right, but the words being spoken aloud along with the witch's expression makes it more real. I shudder at the thought that she could get his power. How badly would the world suffer if this woman managed to absorb the power that flows through Spence right now? I can't imagine the horrors this city would suffer. We can't let that happen, no matter what.

□"And you underestimate me, boy. I will have your power, even if I have to kill you to get it. Or did you miss what happened to your friends?" she pauses and gestures to the three of us as we stand watching this confrontation. "Give me the ring, then we can transfer the rest of your power without any more drama."

□She speaks as if our lives meant nothing. It's painful, but not surprising. Instead of agreeing, Spence throws demon fire at her. When it hits, she's momentarily engulfed in flames. But when they die down, she's barely harmed. "There must be a protection spell in place," I mutter.

□Spence gives a slight nod to let me know he heard what I said and can counter it. I shouldn't be surprised that his hearing is so acute, but I wasn't ready for that. Awe grips me as he battles back and forth against the witch who would have his power.

□"If you want my abilities so badly, perhaps I should share them with you," he says, tossing a different color demon flame at her. This time, Mama Nora screams as the flames eat at her skin, charring and melting parts of her leg, arm, and face away.

□Her screams make me glad that I'm already dead. I can imagine how putrid the smell of burning flesh smells. My heart skips a beat when Spence's reaction is to smirk. Is he enjoying her suffering? I can't help wondering if that's a demon thing, or a this-woman-hurt-me-and-I'm-getting-revenge thing. Either way, it doesn't matter. She deserves everything she gets and then some.

✦

SPENCER

The moment of truth arrives sooner than I'd hoped it would. Even though I manage to hit the witch with my demon flames, she continues to attack me. When she realizes that I'm not backing down, she starts to hurl lightning at the people who are working in the ruins of my home. I can't let her harm them; they're innocent and have nothing to do with this fight.

I pull out the dagger, still trying to decide if it would be better to stab her with it, or stick with my original plan. The moment the witch's eyes meet mine; I know what I have to do.

Without hesitation, I draw my power back into me, not wanting any of it to escape. Then I raise the dagger over my head with my eyes locked on hers. I want her to see the moment she loses this fight. I slam the blade into my chest, straight through my heart, in one smooth motion.

The first thing that steals my breath is the debilitating pain as the meteorite absorbs my power into itself. The next thing that tears my soul from my body is the massive explosion that also destroys my body. From what I read of my father's journal;

I expected that part. What I didn't expect was for Mama Nora to be thrown back into the street and get demolished by a fire truck that was pulling up to help with the search of the ruins.

□I'm not prepared for Kendall's wail when she sees my body explode. Her scream is the single loudest thing I've ever heard, and I'm convinced that if I wasn't already dead, it would have taken me out. I watch with wide eyes as Mama Nora starts to bleed from her eyes, nose, and ears. The noise coming from Kendall doesn't stop until the witch collapses, breaking the privacy spell, she'd cast to keep the humans from seeing us. The moment the spell drops, EMTs rush over to where the old woman dropped.

□"She's dead. How is this possible? There wasn't anyone here a minute ago, and suddenly this old lady pops into existence and dies. This is a bad omen. We need to get out of here," one of them says to the other.

EPILOGUE

KENDALL

The moment Spence's body explodes, I scream, louder than I've ever screamed before. My soul burns with the desire to kill the bitch responsible for all of our deaths. I keep screaming until Spence, Jack, and Murr wrap their arms around me.

"Shhh, love, it's okay. We're with you. She's dead; you can stop now," Spence whispers in my ear, his breath tickling me. How is that possible?

I take a breath, still confused, and tilt my head to look at him. "She's dead?"

He nods, so I turn to look at the other two for confirmation. They nod as well. "You killed her, Kendall," Jack says with a note of awe in his voice.

Murr eases back and takes my hands, pulling me out of the group hug. "It's over now, Kendall. She can't hurt anyone else. Thank you."

It seems strange to me that they're thanking me for taking a life. Even stranger that I don't feel any remorse for killing her. Mama Nora killed each of us either directly or indirectly. She deserved worse than what she got. I only wish I could have tortured her before taking her life.

"Let's get out of here," Spence offers, not seeming bothered by his death. I don't know how he's so calm about everything. Murr freaked out when he died, and I'm pretty sure Jack is still processing. This whole situation is insane. I let Spence lead me away, with Jack and Murr following. Numbness settles over my soul, and I'm not sure I'll ever be the same again.

I shouldn't feel happy that a woman is dead, and I don't, exactly. But I'm not sad at all. I think I would have been upset if someone else had been the one to take her out. I'm glad it was me. That doesn't mean I have any clue about how I did it. Where did that scream come from? No idea. But it was there when I needed it, and that's the important part.

"Where are we going?" Jack asks. For the first time since the drama with the witch started, I hear hope in his voice.

Spence looks at him and smiles. "Home."

I have no idea what he means, but it must be something the three guys have discussed before. Murr and Jack grin in response to Spence's answer. I don't bother to ask where that is, because I'm still wrestling with my lack of remorse and near joy at what I've done.

□"I know it's not much, but for now, it's home. After we've had time to process everything, we can decide where we want to go. I'm pretty sure we can travel fairly easily through ghostly means," Spence explains, leading us to an abandoned warehouse a few blocks away from what used to be our home.

□"This is great," Murr says. It's a nice enough building. There's plenty of space, not that we need a lot. And it's empty; there are no people around to potentially sense or see us.

□I stare out the window, feeling lost and unsure why. Jack slips his arms around me from behind. "What can I do to take your mind off things?" he asks, his lips brushing against my ear. Suddenly, I can think of a ton of things we should do, and none of them involve what just happened.

□"I have some ideas," Spence says, stepping in front of me and sandwiching me between them.

□I look around to find Murr, and his cheeks are the cutest shade of pink. "What about you?" I ask, curious if he's ready for this.

□"I, uh," he stammers.

□"It's okay if you're not ready or interested in group activities," I say with a smirk.

□He looks at me and grins back. "Really? Because I'm not comfortable with that. I don't want you to think I'm not okay with you guys doing stuff, though. I just don't think I can right now." I step away from Jack and Spence, pulling Murr into my arms.

Pressing my lips to his, I kiss him hard. "If you're not comfortable with something, you don't ever have to participate. But are you going to feel left out if we mess around?"

He shakes his head. "I can take a walk."

And just like that, I'm pulled back into the center of a hunk sandwich. This time, Spence steps behind me, and Jack kisses me like he's a dying man and I'm his last meal. I melt between them, unable to handle the stimulation of having both men touch me.

Spence wraps an arm around my waist, pulling me against him. His hard cock presses against my ass, and I gasp, allowing Jack to deepen our kiss. His hands fist in my hair, holding me to him. When he breaks the kiss, I'm breathless and my heart is racing. Confusion grips me for a moment, and I'm not sure how any of this is possible.

"Are you sure you want this?" Spence asks, flicking his tongue against my ear.

I lean back against him. "I do. Everything is weird, though. I feel things I shouldn't—like my heartbeat and breathing."

He smirks against my neck before kissing it. "I thought you'd like it. Turns out I got to keep a little bit of my power after all."

Holy shit. I'm not going crazy, but I don't know if my soul can survive this. I sigh as he continues to kiss and lick my neck, tilting my head to give him better access. Jack's hands slide up my sides and cup my breasts. As overwhelming as these sensations are, I want more. Part of me feels bad that Murr wasn't comfortable enough to join us. Hopefully in the future, he'll change his mind.

□Before I realize what's happening, all three of us are naked. Spence's arm is banded around my chest, under my breasts, holding me to him. Jack drops to his knees and props one of my knees over his shoulder before he runs his tongue along my slit. I groan at how amazing it feels. Then I fist a hand in his hair to keep him in position. My other hand grips Spence's leg, just under his ass.

□I love the feeling of his cock against my ass while Jack's tongue laps at my core. It doesn't take long for me to come on his tongue. Just when I think I'm going to get a break, Spence spins me around, lifts me up and plunges his dick into me. He lifts me up and drops me down, over and over, until I don't think I can take any more. Then he eases us down on the floor, lying on his back, and angles me for Jack to enter my ass.

□Turns out, ghosts don't need lube, and things I didn't expect to feel good, feel incredible. Once Jack is fully sheathed in me, the two of them start moving together, in and out, over and over. I come undone in minutes, crying out in ecstasy. My body feels boneless as they continue to chase their releases. I love being able to bring them pleasure like they do me.

□I know they're getting close when the thrusts turn more desperate and less rhythmic. Somehow, they manage to bring me to the edge again, the three of us falling together. At that moment, Murr tilts my face up to his and kisses me while I'm in the middle of a fantastic orgasm. I don't know when he came back, and he's still fully clothed, but he's here, and that's what matters.

I could get used to this bliss; to our lives being nothing but passion and intimacy; to feeling the love that emanates from the three men I love in return. I finally feel like I'm exactly where I'm supposed to be, and I plan to hold onto this feeling, and them, forever.

what next?

If you enjoyed this book, please consider writing a review. Indie authors, even those with indie publishers, can only thrive if word of their books gets out into the world. Reviews matter. They don't have to be overly detailed, just a sentence or two about what you enjoyed.

Thanks for reading!

ABOUT THE AUTHOR

M.P. Starkweather is a wife, mother, author, poet, casual online gamer, self-proclaimed fan-girl, and full-time nerd. She writes free-form poetry, paranormal romance, sci-fi romance, reverse harem romance, omegaverse romance, and is branching out into contemporary romance. In her free time, she enjoys writing, reading, Dungeons & Dragons, table top games with her husband and friends, and playing with her son. M.P. also enjoys tv, movies, and music across various genres.

To get the most up-to-date information about her latest releases and book signings, check out www.mpstarkweather.com or follow her on your favorite social media site.

ALSO BY M.P. STARKWEATHER

Standalones – Contemporary RH

<u>Finding Fiona</u>

Standalones - Contemporary RH OV

<u>Forsaken Omega</u> – free with newsletter signup

<u>Cold Princes</u>

<u>Knot My Valentine</u>

The Pack Next Door – Contemporary RH OV series

<u>Princess or Knot</u>

<u>Fiancée or Knot</u>

<u>Queen or Knot</u>

<u>The Pack Next Door: The Original Trilogy</u>

<u>Christmas or Knot</u>

Standalones – Paranormal RH

<u>The Wayward Girl</u>

Vampires at Midnight - Paranormal RH series

<u>Blood Moon</u>

<u>Blood Lost</u>

<u>Blood War</u>

<u>Vampires at Midnight: The Complete Trilogy</u>

VaM/HoF Crossover Novella - Paranormal RH

<u>Blood Wolf</u>— free with newsletter signup

Hunters of the Forest - Paranormal RH series

<u>Wolf Bane</u>

<u>Wolf Caged</u>

<u>Wolf Moon</u>

<u>Hunters of the Forest: The Complete Trilogy</u>

Forged by Magic - Sci-fi/Fantasy M/F series

<u>Hidden</u>

<u>Betrayed</u>

<u>Saved</u>

<u>Forged by Magic: The Complete Trilogy</u>

Daydreams and Sunsets - a collection of poetry

<u>Daydreams and Sunsets</u>

www.ingramcontent.com/pod-product-compliance
Lightning Source LLC
Chambersburg PA
CBHW020804310726

48969CB00002B/699